CW00495918

We'll Meet Again

By

Paul Andrews

Grosvenor House
Publishing Limited

This book is published by
Grosvenor House Publishing Ltd
Link House
140 The Broadway, Tolworth, Surrey, KT6 7HT.
www.grosvenorhousepublishing.co.uk

This book is a work of fiction. Any resemblance to
people or events, past or present, is purely coincidental.

A CIP record for this book
is available from the British Library

Paperback ISBN 978-1-80381-873-3
Hardback ISBN 978-1-80381-914-3

INTRODUCTION

This piece of work was started during the Coronavirus pandemic of 2020. It is dedicated to all the unfortunate souls who passed away during this awful time and in particular those in the NHS and care industries who died helping others. Why is it that it was the good people who had to suffer? Why has this virus taken some of the best of humanity?

It is so important in this time to have hope and that is what I have in that death is not the end for these beautiful souls. My religious upbringing taught me to believe that most people that die will live again. It is a wonderful hope to cling on to in this periled world that not only will people live again but it will be in a totally different world where there are no cruel diseases to have to endure. People will stay young and healthy forever in a crime-free and wickedless new world in paradise conditions on this new Earth. God will rule this new Earth and make sure all pain and suffering will be no more. (*Rev. 21.4*)

This piece of work is fictitious, but based on my real beliefs and hopes for the future, as what is life without hope?. We'll meet again is based on my current understanding of the Bible and having been part of my mother's religion as a young child to growing up as a young man it is my most cherished and deepest comfort to have faith that death is not the end. I will see my loved ones again. We'll meet again!

ABOUT THE AUTHOR

Paul was born in 1963 in West Bromwich, but it has only been in the last 10 years that he discovered he had a gift for writing(although Paul did love writing comedy plays for his sisters as a young boy), he firstly began concentrating on writing about his lifelong love of football and fascination with time travel and see where it took him.

Paul's previous work includes **Stop Mark Robins** and **Stop Sergio** (The Visitor from the End of the World). **We'll Meet Again** was motivated by the desire to create comfort for the bereaved during the Covid pandemic, based on creative inspiration from the deeply religious background Paul had as a child and make it into a really entertaining adventure at the same time.

Paul wanted to encourage people to have hope in their hearts based on faith that anybody unfortunate to have passed away will be resurrected. They will get another chance sometime in the future in a much better world where there is no more pain or suffering. It is very comforting for Paul that this is not just pure fiction but something, if you believe in the Bible, will come true one day. There will be a paradise for our loved ones who are no longer with us. This was Paul's understanding from his childhood.

It is Paul's earnest hope you will find this work very uplifting, and as this novel comes in 2 very distinctive halves, it will be so interesting to know which half you the reader prefers. Both halves are very different but put together they compliment each other so well, I hope you will agree with me.

Watch out for my very own favourite chapters which, for me, were so personally gratifying to write and are personal highlights of this novel for me. My personal highlights – Alice is expecting you!, Back before my time, Evie, fatal distraction, If I could turn back time and The beginning of the end.

Please enjoy!

CONTENTS

PART ONE

THE LIGHT

CHAPTER 1

GONE BEFORE MY TIME

30th September 2000

Today was supposed to be one of the best days of my life. It was the day I was going to propose to my gorgeous girlfriend, Amy Jane. She was the love of my life and the centre of my every thought. I couldn't wait to tell her how much I loved her and wanted her to be my wife. I was never going to get that chance; today was the day I was going to die!

I should have realised today was not going to be a good day when my car wouldn't start and it needed to go to a garage. I relied on it to do my very special job. I delivered flowers to mostly very grateful recipients and loved seeing their delightful surprise with such bashful joy etched on their faces. It made me feel so warm and I had my very own and special bouquet ready and waiting to be given to my special girlfriend, Amy Jane, that very night. I was so desperately hoping she was going to say yes to me and make me the happiest person in the world, but alas, all that was imminently awaiting me was the cruel hand of fate as death, my death was going to separate us!

Maybe today would have been a good day to call in sick when my car didn't start. Maybe I wouldn't have been in the wrong place at the wrong time if I had, but I loved my job and didn't want to let my boss, Heather, down in her hour of need. She was a great boss and I was so grateful to have the job so I accepted her offer that her boyfriend, Woolly Bully, could drive me around in getting my deliveries done while my car was repaired. It was just for one day, what could go wrong?. Woolly Bully had only recently passed his driving test but he seemed competent enough, I didn't feel any nerves being driven around by him and it had all gone smoothly. There was one final delivery near Alrewas left to be undertaken and then I was free for the rest of the day and I was dreaming about this very special evening I had planned with Amy Jane when BANG! ....

Woolly Bully had missed a right hand turn into Alrewas and in a panic braked severely when previously going around 40 miles per hour. It meant the car behind crashing into us at speed. Woolly Bully's car had been shunted on a further 30 yards and totally spun sideways as a result of the impact. Shards of glass laid strewn all over the road and there was a body lying face down, motionless, amongst it all.

As anxious bystanders raced to the stricken body to see what they could do to help the poor soul, I could hear crying as it was obvious there was no sign of life as they turned the body over. It was me lying there dead in the road, it was me!! I could see Woolly Bully bleeding profusely and in deep shock, but at least he was alive. It was me who was dead and yet I didn't feel dead.

My body was staring at me all lifeless, It was like I was looking down on it from above and hovering over it. My body was obviously dead but my spirit wasn't. My physical presence had ended but I wasn't gone, I was still here. I could feel overwhelming sadness at how pitiful my once cherished body looked. I was devastated at its demise; there was no life-affirming sparkle or speck of light in the eyes, they had departed and then it dawned on me that I was that speck of light that had departed from my body. I was a spirit all alone in this world without a physical body to reside in. This was an absolute calamity; what was to become of me now?

For seemingly the next few days all I could feel was torment and despair. I had been deprived of my life's greatest wish in marrying Amy Jane and all I could see was how inconsolable and devastated she was on learning about my death. She never knew I was going to ask her to be my wife; she was never going to know! I could see my mum and sisters crying their eyes out at losing me. I could see my very frail father palpably trembling with shock and my poor son, Dean, a very strong young man who had designs of being in the army reduced to wallowing in floods of tears. It was so excruciatingly sad and unbearable to watch. I did not want to continue to bear witness to such suffering; I was suffering as well and if I couldn't be in a physical body anymore, I did not want to be around. It was too much!

It was then I saw the light calling me. It was beckoning me to follow the light. I was being urged to surrender to the light and let it absorb me. Every instinct in my being told me to trust the light and let it take me and it did.

It lifted me from this mortal coil. I was being taken into God's care and put into a peaceful rest but a rest from what?.

My time on this Earth as a 37 year old man was now truly at a premature end. I was truly gone before my time!(but was I?).

Mr Paul Jackson, R.I.P.

CHAPTER 2

PHOENIX

- Revelation 21.1 and 4 -
'And I saw a new Heaven and a new Earth, for the
former Heaven and Earth had passed away.
And He will wipe out every tear from their eyes
and death will be no more.
Neither will mourning nor pain be anymore,
the former things have passed away'

The year 0005 G.K.E (God's Kingdom Era)

"He's alive! ..... He's alive! He is back with us, let us all rejoice" cheered the gathering crowds as a door was swung open in front of me, leaving me totally exposed to the beautiful shimmering sunlight around me.

I was totally confused, totally unaware of my new surroundings and totally unaware of my new reality. Where was I?, What was going on?, I had been in the most blissful and peaceful sleep imaginable but now I was being met by hordes of excitable people all seemingly very pleased to see me. I was being greeted like I was a long-lost friend by these strangers. I did not know where I was but I was now beginning to remember the distressing memories of my previous demise, and was just about to burst into tears when I felt a friendly hand on my left shoulder.

"Welcome back, Paul" said a very familiar and recognisable voice. "I have so missed you, we all have." It was my mum. It felt so reassuring to hear her voice again, but as I turned around to greet her, I was going to get the shock of my new life!

"Mum, you are so young; you look younger than me!, What is going on?, Your hair is the same auburn that I noticed in the photographs in your house; you have no wrinkles whatsoever and look so fresh-faced. You look about 30 years old and in the prime of life. I am so glad you look young but what is happening?".

"I know, it's such a shock", said Mum. "Don't worry, Paul, I will tell you everything. There is so much to tell you but you need to brace yourself".

"Okay" I agreed before noticing a very sprightly man running towards me with great speed. "Is that dad? It's not dad, is it? It can't be, can it?" I yelled. "How can this be, as my dad is not an old man anymore. He was riddled with ailments; he was infirm and had just had a stroke and yet now he is running towards me so fast he looks a young man again, so full of energy. He is like a new man. I think I am going to faint."

"Hello, son," greeted dad. "Welcome back, son. I couldn't wait for this day again to come and now it has. I am so overjoyed you are alive again."

"Can someone please tell me what is going on?" I pleaded. "This is too much for me to take in."

"Sit down, Paul," calmed mum. "I will try and explain. You have been reborn; you have come back from the dead and been born into a world reformed. It is a totally different world to the one you once knew. Your dad passed away in the year 2010; he has been reborn into this world just like you have."

"You died, dad. I am so sorry," I remarked. "I had fears you were suffering badly when I got killed. You lasted another 10 years so you fought hard."

"I did, but when the end came I was ready for it. My body was wracked with disease; it was a merciful release" claimed dad. "I, too, woke up just like you did to this new world and was delighted to feel myself free from all the aches and pains that had afflicted me in my old age. I felt wonderful again and it was so liberating. To see my reflection in a mirror and see my young self looking back at me was so awe inspiring I have to admit I cried."

"I am so glad for you and mum but how has this happened?" I asked.

"I will let your mum answer that," replied dad. "She was there at the end."

"The end of what?" I asked, feeling very confused.

"The End of Days," answered mum. "The end of man's rule on this earth. You could call it Armageddon; It was the final war of humanity; it was good versus evil. The war between good and evil and God was on the side of the good fighting the forces of evil ruled by Satan. There was a choice to be made; you were either on the side of the good or the side of the bad. There was no middle ground, no sitting on the fence. You were either in or out. You were either for God or you weren't. You could recognise God's right to be in charge of this world or you didn't. I did recognise God's right to be in charge as the world was in such a mess at the end. It needed putting right. There was so much wickedness in the world it couldn't continue like that and it didn't. When you got killed I turned to the Bible for comfort and I am so glad I did as it saved my life. It made me aware of what was to come and everything it said has come true. The Bible warned about what would happen, good and bad."

"It sounds very interesting," I agreed. "What did you learn? What did you realise?"

"I learnt God was coming, it was just a question of time. It was not 'if', it was 'when'," answered mum. "There were so many signs if you just cared to look in the Bible. I became on onlooker, a God's onlooker," mum proudly proclaimed.

"Wow! What were the signs that convinced you God was coming?" I asked her.

"There were a lot of signs," remarked mum. "First of all, it was described the Earth would be ruined. I could see the Earth's climate was warming too fast, there was so much angst over climate warming, everybody was worried about sea levels rising, the oceans were full of plastic rubbish, there was too much pollution in the air, lots of animals were on the verge of extinction. It all added up to man ruining the Earth and God calling them to account (*Rev. 11.18*) (*Matthew 24.22*). This was the first red flag but there was also this vivid description of how so many people would behave in the last days. In (*2 Timothy 3*), it said in the last days mankind would be lovers of themselves, lovers of money, self-assuming, haughty, blasphemers, disobedient to parents, unthankful, disloyal, not open to any agreement, slanderers, without self-control, fierce, without love of goodness, having no natural affection, betrayers, headstrong, lovers of themselves rather than lovers of God, puffed up with pride, the list goes on and it was so obvious just how many people were acting like that. It was horrible to see. There was plenty of good people around as well but they were becoming a minority to the selfish, insufferable majority. The Earth was becoming a scary place to live and it had been predicted."

"It certainly sounded horrible," I agreed. "Was there any good news that kept your spirits up? I would have been scared out of my wits if I knew something unpleasant was coming."

"Yes, there was," claimed mum. "When you got killed, I was so heartbroken I was very ill. I needed hope and the Bible gave it to me when I most needed it."

"What was it?" I asked her.

"It said when God won the war and the good defeated the evil, people that had died would be resurrected. They would live again (*John 5.28*). I thought of you and I cried. I wanted to see you again, I wanted to see my long-lost mother alive again. I had this precious gift of hope. I knew death was not the end and not only that, when God won his war against evil man it said the Earth would be transformed, people would be transformed and not suffer pain, tears, outcry or even death anymore (*Rev. 21.4*). It said we would become young again and never have to grow old again. We would become perfect and have abilities that were never thought possible. Look at me and your dad; we are living proof of the Bible coming true," said mum, getting very emotional.

"I am so glad you were one of the good people. I am so glad and relieved you were on the right side," I comforted her before preparing myself to ask the most important question of my new existence, something so profound it would seem like the miracle of my new life would not be worth living if I received a negative answer. So it was, with a massive deep breath, I asked "What about my son, Dean? Is he still alive? Did he come through the Great War between good and evil?"

"Yes, he did, son," was my dad's very gratefully received response. "He's alive and well and is so looking forward to seeing you once he finishes work later and telling you all about how he lived after your unfortunate death. He's been so excited ever since we knew you were coming back."

"Thank God he is still alive. I couldn't have bared it if he wasn't," I sighed with the upmost relief. "I am so looking forward to seeing my son again. I can't believe I am going to see him again after all these years."

"I know, It's great, Paul. I am so happy for the both of you but you need to know his mother, your ex-wife, did not make it past the Great War so please tread carefully on that subject. I also have to tell you your youngest sister did not make it, either. I am so sorry to have to tell you that, Paul but the Great War was brutal and your youngest sister did not want to recognise God and so rebelled and sided with the wrong side. I am so sorry but she was a grown woman with her own free choice and she chose wrong, unfortunately. We all had a free choice; there were winners and losers depending on whether you could accept man couldn't rule or run the Earth properly, so it needed God to step in before it was too late (*Matthew 24.22*). It was said at the time of the Great War that the Earth had reached its tipping point and if it continued a minute longer the planet would not be saved for anybody, good or bad, so it needed Almighty intervention to happen. The rest is history," said mum.

"I can't believe my youngest sister, Lisa didn't make it, I will so miss her. She always had the courage of her convictions, didn't she?, She always knew her own mind and would not compromise for anybody, I'm so gutted she won't be around," I muttered before once more preparing myself to ask about another person I wanted to know if she was still alive. All the mention of mortality amongst a family member had made me feel so nervous at asking this question but I had to know for my own sanity and I was only going to be partially pleased with the answer.

"Mum, you know Amy Jane?, my beloved Amy Jane that I was going to ask to marry me on the very day I died, has she survived?, I need to know so badly, I loved her so much, you know I loved her so much, didn't you? Please tell me she has survived; she is too beautiful to be dead. I couldn't bear it if you told me she is no longer around. Maybe if she has survived I could seek her out and we could begin a beautiful relationship again. I know she is the one for me and will always be the one for me," I said, pleading to be given good news.

"Paul, Amy Jane is still alive. She made it through. She is one of the good people," comforted mum.

"That's brilliant!, I am so relieved, I want to go and see her and tell her I love her," I cheered.

"Paul, calm down please. There's something you need to know," said mum, instantly trying to dampen down my euphoria.

"What's that?" I asked her, suddenly feeling troubled.

"She's married now, She's a married lady, She's off limits I am afraid. I know you loved her but she was only 23 years old when you died so there was so much for her to live for. I know she loved you; she told me so many times, but in the end she had to move on. I am sure you wanted her to be happy, didn't you?. She did meet somebody else, someone younger, but in actual years was closer to her age than you were. I know you looked and acted a lot younger than your age when you were alive but you were 37 years old, so that was quite an age gap, wasn't it?. I am sorry this is not what you want to hear but please be happy for her. Nobody could be sure you would ever live again. Even though the Bible gave clues as what was to come, it never gave the timeframe," said mum.

"I'm ....., I'm ....., I'm so pleased," I said, trying to hide my devastation. It was so fantastic Amy Jane was still alive but she wasn't going to be my girl, she was somebody else's very special girl. This news floored my very soul, it was heart wrenching. I did not know whether to laugh or cry as she was alive; that was most important, but the torment of knowing she loved someone else was something I did not know I wanted to live with.

"She is happy, Paul. I see her here a lot," comforted mum.

"Who is she married to?" I asked her, hardly daring to want to know the answer.

"There is no easy way to tell you this, Paul. Please sit down," insisted mum. "She's ....., she's ....., she's married to Dean. They married in the year 2010, just after your dad passed away."

"Oh my God!, No!, Please tell me this is a bad dream; this is too much. You are telling me my beloved Amy Jane is married to my son. This is unbearable!, I wish

I was still asleep. At least I would not have to face this agony," I cried.

"You will get used to it, Paul, you will in time," comforted mum. "I know you are upset as I know you loved her and she did love you but your son was there for her when she was at her lowest ebb. There was even a time Amy Jane was thinking of suicide so your son was a lifesaver. Please don't be harsh on your son; he loves you and is so happy you are alive again. He is dreading the moment he has to explain how he is now married to your greatest love. I guess this will be the ultimate test of a father to son relationship now, won't it?"

"It sure will be," I confirmed.

"There are so many beautiful girls in this New Order, new Earth," soothed mum. "You won't be single for long. You're a good-looking man, you will be spoilt for choice."

"But there is none as beautiful as Amy Jane," I argued. "There is only one Amy Jane; she is priceless, the ultimate princess."

"I am afraid she will never be yours now. I am sorry to be so blunt, but it is how it can only be now," replied mum, very bluntly.

"Don't rub it in, mum. I know it would put my son and me at war so I know Amy Jane is off limits but you seem so unequivocal, like you are almost warning me about something. What do I need to know?" I asked her.

"There are rules now, very sacred rules now," warned mum. "You must not covet another man's wife, You must not commit adultery, You must not commit fornication or have sex with anybody that is not your wife or husband, It is completely forbidden. The good news is we are all becoming perfect with perfect minds, it shouldn't be hard to obey the rules; these are God's rules, they must be obeyed. Even thinking about having relations outside your marriage is breaking these sacred rules but having a perfect mind will make this perfectly easy to adhere to. When the good defeated the evil with God's help and God began his rule, new scrolls were opened. It was like the 10 Commandments reimposed and adapted for the modern world. It was for our ultimate benefit, a price for our perfect new lives. It wasn't too much to ask. We had to respect God and show that we cared for his authority to rule over us."

"What happens if a person wilfully transgresses these new rules?" I asked.

"That person or people would be removed from this New Order. They would be returned to eternal sleep, They would never live again," revealed mum. "Can you see now that you will have to accept the fact Amy Jane is now your son's wife and it will stay that way forever. It is ordained, you have no choice but to find your own special person," warned mum.

"I feel sick," I said. "I know I will have to get used to it but it won't be easy. I'm not looking forward to seeing them together, that is for sure."

"You can't or must not let it eat you up," remarked mum. "This is not the way things work in this New Order. You will meet someone else; I guarantee it."

"I will just have to trust you on that," I stated.

"I know it's not easy, son," dad added. "I can testify to that."

"What do you mean, dad?" I asked him, feeling very puzzled.

"I am no longer married to your mum," he answered. "When I passed away in 2010 so did the marriage to your mum. You've heard the saying 'til death do us part'; well, my death did part us, I'm afraid. Your mum has remarried, so I, too, have had a very painful reintroduction to a new life. I was mortified and didn't know how to react but I had no choice. I did adapt; I've got a new lady that loves me, your mum has moved on, you can too."

"I am so glad you were able to move on, I so admire you for that," I replied. "One thing that his puzzling me is how come you came back before me when you died 10 years after me? How does that work?"

"I'll let your mum answer that," dad replied.

"The Great War between good and bad happened in the year 2033," revealed mum. "That was the day and year the world you once knew finished and all the evil and selfish people and the people that didn't accept God were eradicated from the Earth (*Psalms 37.10 and 11*). I was now 90 years old and so glad I never knew what it was like to die, although I had terrible arthritis. By now, your son, by the way, was 45 years old and Amy Jane 52 years old, so they were in middle age now. As soon as the evil people had gone and been removed and God had started his rule, I immediately started getting better. My ageing process was in full reverse and in 5 years I got to the person that I look today. I feel and look just 30 years old. I was so ecstatically relieved to feel all my aches and pains just disappear. Your son lost 15 years in age in just over a year and Amy Jane took 2 years to reclaim her former youth and beauty. It was wonderful to see and then once everybody was back to being their prime selves, it was time to start preparing for all former departed loved ones to be resurrected, starting from the most recent deceased to the most ancient.

"Your dad died in 2010 so he was reborn before you by about 1 year. You have now been reborn and you died in the year 2000 and it's brilliant that you are here. I can't wait until I can see my dead mum and dad again; you know how devastated I was when my own mum died in 1965 – you were only a little nipper. I know it will be a little more time before she is reborn, as at the current rate it should be in two years' time but I am going to cry so much when I see her, I know I will and I think it's mind-blowing to realise there will be people being eventually reborn that were alive thousands of years ago. They will need the most help to adjust to this new Earth as they have been asleep for so long and everything is going to come as a fundamental shock to them. I can't wait to talk to them and ask them what it was like to live all that time ago. It gives me goose bumps just thinking about it."

"It does sound awe inspiring," I agreed. "By the way, dad said you married again, who is he?"

"His name is Ewan, Ewan the Wise," answered mum. "He is an Elder and he is such a lovely man."

"Yes, he is, son," added dad. "He is a very gentle and lovely man. Your mum did well; I hold no grudges as it has all worked out for the best."

"What is an Elder?" I asked.

"An Elder is part of the ruling class of men appointed by God and under direct jurisdiction of the Angels. You could say they are like line managers. It is their duty to direct the teaching work for the newly reborn and the Unrighteous Class of people that survived the Great War. Although they had accepted God's rule they hadn't yet attained the privileges of the Righteous Class whom had loyally been spreading God's word before the war came. They had put their money where their mouth was. Do you know how much ridicule and even persecution came from the evil ones in the time of the End? It was horrendous. As a result of supreme loyalty under extreme duress there are a group of people in this New Order that have already attained Righteous Class status. I am one of those people. Everybody will have to attain Righteous status before the end of 1,000 years or ......"

"Or what?" I urged.

"The people that haven't attained Righteous status by the end of 1,000 years will not be able to live on. There will be a second and permanent death for those people," was mum's startling reply. "But don't worry, Paul. You will be alright, I am sure of it. You will have a perfect mind in a perfect body. There is no need to worry; I am sure you will pass the test when it comes to it. Your dad was in the same boat; he had still failed to attain Righteous status until recently. He is learning all the time and you will, too. I am a teacher now; all the Righteous Classes are teachers and the Elders are super teachers. They are the ones you really have to impress at first. Ewan The Wise, my husband, is the Elder I hope you get to be under his control as he is the gentlest. He is a kind man. You do have an acclimatisation period, a settling in period before you get the conditioning work so please get to know this new world better. I will help you; you are my son. I want what is best for you, you do know that, don't you?"

"Yes, of course," I replied, but now I was starting to wonder what had I been reborn into. It was starting to feel a little bit repressive and even chilling. To be honest, I wasn't sure I even wanted to be here and yet here I was. It was wonderful to see my mum and dad looking young again but they weren't even married to each other anymore and my beloved Amy Jane was seemingly eternally unobtainable with my son. Was there anything good about being alive again?. Like a phoenix, I had risen from the flames only to find uncertainty. Was I good enough for this New Order? Did I even want to be good enough for this New Order?

As my mum invited me round to her home, what was going to be my next shock?

CHAPTER 3

WELCOME TO PARADISE

"Wow!, Your house is so beautiful, it is like a palace," I enthusiastically proclaimed. "You've done so well, mum. I love it. How did you manage to get such a nice place?"

"I guess I'm a lucky lady," answered mum. "It helps being in the favoured class I suppose and I struck lucky meeting Ewan as it was his house. The Righteous Class do tend to be in the nicer houses; it is like we have earned the right, almost."

"It is wonderful alright," I remarked." I have to admit everywhere looks wonderful as far as I can see. This new world seems like it has been transformed into a paradise, It is like I am in a giant Garden of Eden."

"That's right, Paul," nodded mum. "When God stepped in after the Great War the Earth was in a terrible state. The polar ice caps were melting prolifically so sea levels were extremely high. Some island countries and low coastal areas had been wiped out completely. Climate change had seen whole continents turning into inhospitable deserts. It was so bleak it was unbelievable and horrible to witness. At a stroke, God turned it around. The deserts retreated until they no longer existed, the Sahara is a distant memory; it is now a green plain. Everywhere is nice and sunny but not too hot. God transformed the whole Earth; there is no inhospitable place anymore in the world. From the top of the highest mountain to the depth of the deepest ocean to the poles of the Arctic and Antarctic everything has been rewritten for all mankind to enjoy. There is such a luscious abundance of foliage everywhere with glorious palm trees all around. It feels like Heaven on Earth and it is wonderful to exist in it. Would you like to have a look around in the garden, Paul?"

"Yes, of course," I replied.

"Don't be alarmed by anything you see there," said mum.

"What do you mean?" I asked her, so intrigued by what she meant. I was so confused but then I saw something lurking at the bottom of her garden.

"Is that a lion, It is a lion!, Bloody hell, you've got a lion in your garden! What is going on?"

"Please don't swear, Paul. It is forbidden" warned mum. "I told you not to worry, it is normal. The lions are everywhere but don't worry, they won't hurt you. No animal will ever hurt a human now., they are all tame, it is the new way of things. Don't you think it's magical?. God has reprogrammed all the animals not to fear us anymore or want to attack us anymore. A little boy or girl can ride on the back of a saltwater crocodile and not be harmed. You can go in the sea and play with a group of great white sharks; it is wondrous (*Isiah 11, 6-9*). Would you like to stroke the lion? It is coming over to us."

"Er, I don't know," I stuttered. I am not used to this, Lions are supposed to be ferocious, aren't they?, I don't feel comfortable with this."

"Oh Paul, don't be such a wuss," laughed mum. "Look, the lion is tilting his head for you to stroke it. He wants you to tickle his chin. Go on, be brave; you won't regret it."

"Wow!, I can't believe I am doing this," I said as the lion duly licked my hand.

"You will find the relationship between animals and humans has been transformed beyond your wildest imagination. Nobody in this New Order eats meat anymore. No animal is killed anymore. It is forbidden. We all eat nutritious plant diets now so there is no need for animals to fear us like they once did. They have regained their trust of humans. They are now our best friends. Isn't it wonderful?"

"Yes, I guess so," I remarked. "I will have to get used to no bacon sandwiches in this New Order, or a KFC, won't I?"

"Definitely," remarked mum. "You won't find a KFC or a McDonalds in this world."

"I am guessing there is a lot of things I was used to in my time that are not here now, aren't there?" I asked mum.

"I know what you are going to say next," said mum. "You were football mad, You lived for football and the Villa, didn't you?. Well, I'm sorry, Paul, There is definitely no Premier League in this New Order. We all support God now. Football and all competitive sport are outlawed. We can play sport for fun but that is all there is."

"I was dreading you saying that," I said feeling very underwhelmed. I had lived for sport; where was the fun in a world without the Villa?.

"There is quite a lot of things around in the world you knew that are not around or necessary anymore," replied mum.

"Like what?" I asked her.

"There are no doctors, no dentists, no hospitals as there is no need for them. Nobody feels pain anymore as we have perfect bodies. There is also no need for cars, trains, ships and aeroplanes anymore, they are redundant and that is a good thing as they produced such a big carbon footprint that jeopardised the very future of the Earth in the time of the End," revealed mum. "There is also no phones or computers."

"How does everybody get around, then?" I asked her, feeling very puzzled. "How does everybody communicate?"

"We teleport, Paul. There are so many wonderful things you haven't yet realised about our new perfect bodies" explained mum. "Did you ever realise us humans utilised only a fraction of what our brains were capable of?. Now that we are perfect, we have much more access to the full power of our wonderful brains. They are a miracle of creation. The major thing that came to us was the sheer power of thought. You can make things happen by the power of thought alone, Isn't that great?. So, if you want to be somewhere you just open up your imagination and make it so by the power of focus and concentration on that thought and then the will to execute that thought. In essence, you are that thought and that thought becomes reality. I do have to tell you that it takes graduation to the Righteous Class to have full unblocked potential of our brains but the Unrighteous still enjoy restricted benefits to their brains' potential as they learnt to develop and adapt to this new world. It gives the Unrighteous extra motivation to adapt quicker. We can also transmit and communicate with each other by thought alone, so you can be in direct contact with another person hundreds or even thousands of miles away. Dean and Amy Jane will be here in a minute, Are you ready for them?, Can you handle this moment?, It will be so overwhelming, won't it? After all this time for you, I imagine your mind has not yet grown full discipline, It takes time in the New Order to develop full discipline. That's why your mind can't be given unrestricted access to everything it can do until you reach maturity in this New Order and that means Righteous status."

"I understand. It does give me motivation as everything you described does sound incredible," I replied. "I have got to be honest; I feel like a nervous wreck right now. I have such mixed emotions. I love my son dearly but he is married to my greatest love, It is so gut wrenching."

"This is going to be a big first test for you to see how quickly you might be able to adapt, Paul," said mum.

"How long is it before they are here?, Can you sense them coming?" I asked her.

"I have received their thoughts, Paul. They want you to be prepared for their arrival," revealed mum. "They will appear in 30 seconds. There won't be a knock on the door; as you can see I don't have a door. Nobody needs security in the New Order; crime is a thing of the past. It was the way of the evil ones and they are no more. Nobody commits crimes of any sort in the New Order. We have perfect minds; we know the difference between right and wrong. There is only right now, but if anybody ever did commit a wrong they would be removed from the New Order with great haste to eternal death. It is so liberating and wonderful to know nobody will ever steal from you or do the horrible things evil people were doing, such as murder, in the time of the End. They are here, Paul. Are you ready to greet them?"

"I can't see them," I was just about to say when Dean and Amy Jane just materialised in front of me making me almost faint with shock.

"Dad! Dad! I can't believe I can see you again," greeted a highly emotional son. "I've missed you so much. I have been waiting for this day to come for such a long time. I can hardly believe you are now here. I love you, dad."

"Dean, just look at you! You are so grown up, so different, so impressive. I've missed so much, haven't I? You were only a teenager when I died; I've missed seeing you blossom into the man you now are. You look a picture of health; you are handsome. I am so glad you didn't take after me," I joked." I will give credit to your mum for that. You look perfectly sculptured; you look a great catch and just look at you – you are a married man. There is so much to learn and catch up on, I've missed so much; I've missed you so much".

"Don't worry, dad. I will tell you everything," comforted Dean. "There is so much to tell you."

"You're not wrong," I replied. "I can see you have a lovely wife. Congratulations, Dean, you look a beautiful couple."

"Hello again, Paul," said Amy Jane. "It is beautiful to see you again. I am so happy that you are alive again."

"It's beautiful to see you as well," was my very bittersweet reply as the awkwardness I felt in my soul was causing all sorts of aching in my heart. "Dean has chosen very well, hasn't he?"

"You're making me blush," replied Amy Jane bashfully.

"Sit down, dad. I will try and explain how my life has panned out without you in my life," encouraged Dean.

"Dean was really ill when you died," interrupted mum. "For a long time, he was inconsolable and we were really worried about him. You were his best friend; you were the one that played sport with him, especially tennis. You were the one who took him to watch Premier League matches, you were the one that took such interest in his junior soccer sides and you were the one that took him on such nice holidays. From teaching Dean how to swim and ride a bike as a young boy It was obvious just how much love you had for your son which you gave with such joy. It took your death for Dean to realise what he had lost. Teenagers can take their parents for granted, can't they?"

"It's true, dad," Dean agreed. "I did take you for granted. I always thought you would be here for me. I was devastated you weren't here anymore. I wish I had told you how much I loved being your son; you were a wonderful dad."

"Thank you for such kind words, Dean. It is making me feel very emotional," I replied. "The day you were born was the greatest day of my life and will always remain so. I couldn't believe how lucky I was to have you as my son. I was the luckiest person in the world. You made me happy beyond words. I need to know how you moved on with your life and ended up like you are now, as I have to be honest, I am amazed, if not a little disappointed you have ended up married to a girl I held very dear."

"I knew you would be," replied Dean. "I was dreading today in that respect but I will explain to you what happened to me after you died. At the age of 15 I joined the army. It was the best thing that could have happened to me as it made me become a man instead of a boy. It taught me how to be strong both mentally and physically, It helped me let go of the terrible pain of your death, dad."

"That's very impressive," I admitted. "I am proud you were tough enough for the army."

"I earnt great money and a lot of kudos being in the army. I began to live hard and play hard," said Dean.

"By that he meant he became a babe magnet, isn't that right Dean?" interrupted mum. "Girls were falling over themselves to be with him. He was loving them and leaving them, weren't you, Dean?"

"I was living the dream," admitted Dean.

"But then came your posting to Afghanistan, didn't it?" mentioned mum. "Tell your dad how that came about."

"In September 2001, a year after your death, the Twin Towers skyscrapers in New York were attacked and demolished by suicide bombers that were part of an organisation called Al-Qaeda. They were religious terrorists that had bases in Afghanistan. War was basically declared there and then. Being in the army, I ended up in Afghanistan. It was a hellhole, a living hellhole, a very hostile and alien environment for a young man to be a long way from home," said Dean.

"We were all worried sick for Dean," admitted mum. "There were a lot of casualties out there, either people dying or people being maimed. It was clear, even back then, the world was starting to go nuts. It made me think something was brewing. First it was Afghanistan, then it became Iraq and then worst of all, Islamic State came into existence. I am so glad Dean had left the army by then."

"What was the Islamic State?" I asked her.

"They were truly evil and barbaric," answered mum. "They slaughtered their enemies, they beheaded innocent people or burnt people alive. They were extremely evil and dangerous and a symbol of a world spinning out of control. They manipulated and brain-washed people on social media."

"What is social media?" I asked.

"I will let Dean answer that one," said mum.

"When you died, dad, technology went crazy," revealed Dean. "Everybody started having computers or laptops, our phones began to get better and better, they could do everything on them. Young people in particular became crazy to interact with each other online. There was a site called Facebook that was very popular; it became a major part of people's lives. It virtually took over people's lives as it became bigger and bigger. Everybody wanted and owned a smartphone and to be on Instagram, Whatsapp or Twitter."

"Twitter? That sounds like something a bird does," I commented. "It sounds crazy; was all this technology a good thing?"

"It was good and bad," explained Dean. "The good thing was you could Google anything; if you wanted to know something all you had to do was Google."

"Google?, What's that?" I asked.

"Google was an incredible search engine that could virtually answer any question you wanted," explained Dean.

"It sounds fantastic," I replied. "It sounds like I really missed out, didn't I?"

"You would have thought so, but people became obsessed with technology; it is almost like they sold their souls for it. I loved it, I admit it, but it wasn't healthy," said Dean.

"It helped the rise of the evil ones," interrupted mum. "Technology could be a force for good and lots of good things could be done online but there was such a lot of darkness online. You know about how the Bible described how lots of people would become in the end, (2 timothy 3) well, they were all to be found lurking on the Internet. It was the evil people's favourite battleground; it's where paedophiles lurked in anonymity, it is where crooks lurked as well. It was clear the Internet greatly accelerated the day of the Great War; I am convinced of that. People, vulnerable people, could be bullied online or even encouraged to take their own lives; it was called 'trolling'. People could be brainwashed with false propaganda; that's how the Islamic State operated. It was brutal, wasn't it, Dean?"

"I came off it in the end as I could see so much badness was on it," revealed Dean. "Something in my gut was telling me I needed to get off it if I wanted to live; It was a gut feeling I had but I did it."

"You did meet Amy Jane online though, didn't you, Dean? Tell your dad about it," urged mum.

"It was just after grandad died in 2010 that we married but it was around two years prior to that I noticed Amy Jane's profile online and she was in trouble; she was really struggling with life," revealed Dean.

"That's right, Paul. I was at my lowest ebb; I really needed someone," admitted Amy Jane. "I didn't have a boyfriend for so long after you died because I missed you so much and then eventually I had a very bad relationship where I was abused. I didn't know if I wanted to live anymore. I had moved away from the area and hardly knew anyone as my boyfriend at that time had been very controlling. I moved into a refuge but I was still so vulnerable and lonely. I spent a lot of time online and eventually Dean found my profile online and we grew fond of each other over time. Dean was my knight in shining armour in the end and from out of it grew love. It was very strange falling in love with your son and I never would have wanted in a million years to hurt you as I loved you as well but you were dead. It wasn't certain you would ever live again; all we had was hope. Life is precious; you have to make the most of it. Sometimes you have to live in the present, it's not all about the future."

"I didn't want to fall in love with Amy Jane," added Dean. "I knew how special she was to you but the bond between us became too great to ignore, too great to resist. I hoped I would see you again but I couldn't be sure I would. I love you dad and I know you seeing me with Amy Jane must be so hard for you to get your head around but we were there for each other in the time of the End and I think if that hadn't been the case you might not be seeing either of us now as the world had become so bleak."

"I think I can begin to understand but I am not going to lie, this is hurting me so much right now," I replied. "I do love you son, I really do, but I am going to need time to get my head around it. My head is spinning with everything that is going on; I need time. It is so weird dating was done through technology but I guess it was technology that saved Amy Jane, wasn't it?"

"It was, dad," confirmed Dean. "I would never have known just how sad she was without it. Technology would have blown your mind in the end; we could do so much that you could have only dreamed of before you died. There was virtual reality where you could be anywhere you wanted but you needed the headsets to do it, the special headsets. That was thought miraculous but look at us now; we don't need any headsets to experience virtual reality and we don't need smartphones anymore. We have our perfect enhanced brains that can instantly project us into any reality; we can teleport anywhere instantly. We can read each other's thoughts if we want to or are allowed to. I know what you have been thinking without you even talking, so does your mum, so does Amy Jane. We all know how hurt you are feeling but you will get over it, I promise. You will find another special girl in this New Order. I can't wait for you to achieve Righteous status just as your mum, Amy Jane and myself have. There is such joy to be had in being a teacher, we are all teachers. It is the instruction of the Righteous Class; it is what we have been told to do."

"It sounds all very aspirational," I remarked. "At the minute I guess I am Unrighteous Class; I feel Unrighteous. What does that mean? What does that entail? What is my role right now?"

"You have only just been reborn," said mum. "It takes time to adjust to the new world, to get used to your new perfect body and perfect mind. It takes time to get to know God and what he wants from you in return. You have to learn to gain knowledge at what it takes to flourish in this New Order under God's love and authority. You have to earn that badge; we all have and are Righteous Class. You will in time, it just takes time. Your dad has been alive again for one year and he is on the verge of graduation. It will be so wonderful to see him baptised as a mark of that graduation and he can be on our level again and safe to take the 1,000 year test we all have to pass to claim eternal salvation."

"What's that?" I asked mum.

"At the end of 1,000 years Satan the Devil will be let loose to test us once again to see if we are worthy of eternal life. We have to resist him for one more time to claim this precious prize. If we don't, we will lose our lives forever. You have to be in the Righteous Class to take this test as all remaining unrighteous people will have failed to graduate in time and they will perish forever. So you can see graduation is mandatory if you want to live forever. The good news is you have nearly 1,000 years to achieve it," revealed mum.

"Thanks for that, mum," I replied. "No pressure then. What jobs do the Unrighteous Class do in this New Order?"

"Most of the Unrighteous Class are cultivators, they cultivate the land. It is hard but it is rewarding. You also have mandatory Bible study at Theocratic School with a member of the righteous every lunchtime and every single person on this new Earth goes to Thanksgiving and prays to God at 7 pm every single day without fail," answered mum. "You will get one day off each week to enjoy and explore your new capabilities once you make progress and I am sure you will make progress. I know all this might sound hard and maybe a little unfair, but it isn't when you weren't around at the time of the End like we were. We really had to endure and show faith and courage. All of us really earned our stripes and our survival, so it is fair that were given Righteous status straightaway."

"I can see that," I said. "Just how bad did it get in the end? Maybe it will help me understand even better how you needed to be there for each other."

"We were all part of God's Onlookers for a start, so a lot of the world hated us. We were the ones trying to warn people and most of them didn't like it or take any notice. That wasn't nice. There was still a lot of other decent people on the Earth as well as us and in the year 2020 we all, as humanity, suffered a terrible virus called Covid 19. This was a first great test that gave everybody a chance to show what they were all about. There was basically two types of people; there were selfish people, the people that only cared about themselves. They epitomised everything mentioned in *2 Timothy 3*. They were disobedient, they hoarded, they capitalised on the virus with greed, they were uncaring, without self-control, they were puffed up with their own importance, whereas there were the selfless people; they were the ones that obeyed the rules for the safety of themselves and others. They shared, they cared and even looked after the vulnerable. Some in the care sector and the NHS actually died and gave their lives in an ultimate sacrifice. God didn't forget those people; they are all alive again now. Their lives are restored. Isn't that great? God saw who was selfless and who was selfish. It was a precursor of what was to come at a later date, the Great War. A lot of sorting needed to happen when God won; the good had to be separated from the bad (*Matt 25.32-46*). The virus of 2020 was a dummy run; people had the chance to change if they wanted to, but most of the selfish people didn't, alas," explained mum.

"Why do you think that was?" I asked her.

"Complacency, I guess," answered mum. "Science cured the first virus; science was wonderful and I think most people relaxed. The greedy evil ones continued to flourish, the bad seemed to get away with so much so what encouragement was there for them to change?.

In the year 2030 there was this message that appeared everywhere as if by magic. You couldn't miss it, nobody could miss it, on television, on every phone, on posters and billboards. It transposed itself; it was a warning message."

"What did it say?" I asked mum.

"It said, 'now the works of the world were manifest, they were fornication, uncleanliness, loose conduct, idolatry, spiritism, enmities, strife, jealousy, fits of anger, contentions, divisions, sects, envies, drunken bouts, revelries and things like these. I forewarn you those that practice such things will <u>not</u> inherit God's Kingdom.' (*Gal 5.19*). It also followed that by giving another cryptic clue. 'Those who are sewing with a view to their spirit will reap everlasting life from that spirit'."

"Wow! That is so striking," I remarked. "It was a massive warning, wasn't it? How did it go down with the masses?"

"A lot of people just ignored it; it was to be for their peril," mum answered. "But I knew the world was in trouble and having studied the Bible, I knew all the signs were beginning to come true. The world was heating up and it was so full of wickedness the message had to be true. It actually said it was a forewarning but people, at least most of them, didn't want to take any notice. The message was mocked all around the world but they were definitely not laughing by the year 2033. It was now far too late for them; they had not repented in time."

"What happened in 2033?"

"That was the final year of man's rule. The evil ones were removed. First there was a massive cosmic storm, the like that had never been witnessed before. It was like a massive wrath was exploding from the Heavens (*Matthew 24.29*). God made his presence known to everyone on the Earth. A lot of man's rulers did not want to give up their right to rule; they tried to fight but to no avail. They were rebuffed. A new virus was then released into the atmosphere of the Earth; it attacked only the evil ones and the selfish ones and the ones that didn't want to have God ruling the Earth. This virus, unlike Covid19 previously was merciful as it came from God. It just put the evil ones into a permanent sleep; it killed them, but they didn't feel pain. I suppose that is what separates good from evil and that is mercy. The evil had to die for the good to live on in peace but they didn't suffer in terms of pain."

"Genius," I remarked. "God is a genius. It was such the perfect and fairest way, wasn't it?"

"It had to be done," admitted mum. "The evil was so bad in the end it had to be eradicated for the sake of the whole Earth. It was said if God did not step in, no flesh at all would be saved (*Matthew 24-22*). The evil ones hated the good people; they wanted to kill us in the end. I had faith God was coming but it was still so scary seeing the sun darkened and the moon and stars falling from Heaven."

"I am so glad now I was at rest in sleep," I admitted. "I do have renewed respect for anybody who lived through and survived that; I wouldn't have wanted to witness all that."

With that, I made my peace with mum, Dean and Amy Jane. I wanted to see my dad now; I wanted to catch up with him as I had only seen him briefly so far. What was his life like in the New Order? I wasn't prepared for some of his answers as it made me aware in no uncertain terms I was going to be in for the hardest ride of my life. This perfect world, with perfect bodies, would come at a price. I had just made my reacquaintance with my mum, my son and Amy Jane and it was so surreal seeing them all again after such a long rest in death it hadn't dawned on me that I couldn't take it for granted I could just see them when I wanted from now on. There was no such thing as a free lunch; I was going to find out I had to earn my right to be on their level if I ever wanted to enjoy something that should be automatic - family time. What rude awakenings were awaiting me?

CHAPTER 4

DAD

Arriving at my dad's place, it was obvious it was a much more modest dwelling, not much bigger than a glorified hut. It was a very humble place that was in such stark contrast to the grandeur of my mum's place, but it felt compellingly homely all the same.

It was so strange to see dad in such small surroundings, as in his previous life, he had been a very successful businessman and provided a fantastic standard of living for my mum, my two sisters and myself. We were all very proud of him and very grateful. To give us a house that had an indoor swimming pool complete with sauna was testament to how well he did in life. My son, Dean, hero-worshiped him. My dad enabled us to have such wonderful memories as a family growing up. It was then the full realisation of my mum and dad not being married anymore hit home to me; it made me feel so sad. I was glad mum was happy but was my dad really happy as well? I really hoped he was as he deserved to be happy.

"Hello, dad. I am so glad to see you. Can I come in?" I asked.

"Of course, son, it is wonderful to see you too. It will be great to talk to you," replied dad.

"I still can't get over how youthful you look. It is so fantastic to see you as a healthy young man and not suffering like you were when I died. You're the same age as me now; it is so weird as you are my dad. It's like we are on the same level now but you will always be my dad. That can never change," I said, feeling highly emotional.

"That is lovely of you to say, son," replied dad. "You will have me crying if you're not careful and that is not a good look, is it?"

"I don't think I ever saw you cry except when grandad died," I mentioned. "You were always very strong, you kept your feelings in. You were such a traditional man, so full of inner resolve but you never showed much emotion. It is like you are a different person, you seem a lot freer. I like it."

"Thanks, son," replied dad. "But I am so grateful to be alive again and back to being young again and in such good health. I have learnt to appreciate just how precious good health and a youthful body is. When I was alive before it was like I was just existing, not living. All my focus and concentration and worries were about financial security and making progress in the world without truly appreciating what it meant to be myself, I was too busy living life at a thousand miles an hour. I love this new world; all our cares and worries have been taken away. I definitely think it has moulded my character for the better. I think it is down to the perfecting process."

"I love it that you seem so happy," I remarked. "I wanted to take this chance to tell you how much I loved and appreciated you for everything you did for our family. I died before I could express just how much I respected you. I guess I was just too preoccupied with my own life to recognise what you gave for us and then it was too late, I wasn't here anymore. You were a wonderful dad, so generous and giving. I am so glad we all have a second chance."

"I am glad too," responded dad. "You were a great son, Paul. I loved that you caddied for me when I couldn't walk properly anymore. I loved my golf, didn't I? I lived for golf and for you to give up your Sundays so I could still play in my fourballs meant so much to me despite my dodgy knees. I know I had to give it up in the end because of my health, but I also loved the way you helped look after me in my old age when I really needed it. I loved being your dad just as I loved being a dad to your two sisters. I loved being married to your mum; I loved her. I did everything because I loved you all."

"I feel really sad you are not still together," I admitted. "Are you really okay that mum has a new husband? It must have been such a shock to you."

"It was, son, I won't lie to you. I was heartbroken when I realised she was no longer mine. I felt like I didn't want to be here, I didn't want to be awake," dad admitted. "But things do get better; there is a brighter side of life to grab hold of. I adjusted eventually. It did really hurt; it hurt very badly but a year on I am on the verge of Baptism into the Righteous Class and have a new love called Pammie. We are going to get married as soon as I get Baptised; I am so excited. Pammie is getting baptised the same day as me. It is a good job she is or I would have had to wait for her."

"What do you mean?" I asked dad.

"Righteous Class people are forbidden to have relationships romantically with Unrighteous Class people. So, if I graduated before her, I would have to wait for her and vice versa. I would have been so gutted if I had been forced to give her up, she is my world now. I was so lucky that we both joined Theocratic School at the same time and formed a great relationship straight away. She died in the year 2010, the same as me. She was a big smoker apparently and died of throat cancer. I couldn't imagine her as an old lady that she once was as she is so full of verve and vitality. She is so bubbly and I adore her. I can't wait for us to marry so we can make love and even kiss. I so want that," groaned dad.

"You haven't even kissed her?" I said, feeling really shocked.

"It is forbidden," answered dad. "You can't have any relations at all with the opposite sex physically if you are not married and that means kissing and cuddling as well. I won't lie to you; it has been my biggest test in this New Order. It has been incredibly frustrating but you have to obey the rules. The positives do outweigh the negatives though in this New Order but it is no coincidence everybody that has formed a relationship in the Unrighteous Class and has graduated into Righteous Class rush like crazy to get married as they are bursting with affection for each other. Tony the Hawk was my guiding Elder and he has the most purest standards of them all. He is almost puritanical but he kindly let me be able to hold hands with Pammie as he could see we liked each other. It certainly is an incentive to progress when you like a girl and that's what I did. Thankfully Pammie was just as keen to progress. We were lucky, as Tony the Hawk is usually very unwilling to have anything remotely friendly going on when he is teaching. They call him 'the Hawk' as he can spot any indiscretion, however miniscule, a mile off with hawklike intensity. I hope you avoid Tony the Hawk as your guiding Elder."

"He does sound very strict," I agreed. "What is Theocratic School like? Is it hard?"

"It is hard but I found it enjoyable in the end because of Pammie," answered dad. "If you need any support or advice you know where to come; I am there for you. I just hope you don't get Jefferson as your guiding Elder as he is extreme; he will work you to death. He is remorseless. He is nicknamed 'the Pope' such was his sense of almost divine importance but don't you dare call him that in his presence. His students worked twice as many hours as anybody else at Theocratic School and his graduation approval rate of his students was far less than the other Elders. I hope you get Ewan the Wise or Levi if you get the chance as that is your best hope of attaining fast approval for the Righteous Class."

"What do they teach you?" I asked dad.

"They train you in the fruits of the spirit to maximise the new potential you have in your perfect body and mind. They teach you how to imitate godlike standards in your life; they teach you what God wants and expects from you from now on. You are taught every single meaning in the Bible and how to pass it on to others when you reach Righteous Class as there are so many people like you and me that are going to be reborn from the dead and need teaching about what is expected of them. So essentially you have to gain knowledge, intensive knowledge and then be able to pass on that knowledge. You have to have shown you can exhibit mastery in all the individual fruits of the spirit to gain approval for baptism into the Righteous Class," revealed dad.

"What are those fruits of the spirit?" I asked him.

"They are love, joy, peace, self-control, kindness, mildness, goodness, long-suffering and finally faith (*Galatians* 6.8). That is the hardest fruit to master and the hardest test to pass," said dad.

"Why is that, dad?" I said.

"You will be given a test that requires faith to pass and acquire the faith gold standard," answered dad.

"What did you have to do?" I asked him.

"My test of ultimate faith involved drinking a glass full of hydrochloric acid. My guiding Elder, Tony the Hawk, poured it out in the glass. It was frothing, it was steaming. It looked terrifying and utter madness to put that drink into my mouth. I could literally imagine it completely burning my insides out and melting me. I'll be honest with you, son, I waivered; I didn't want to do it but I was told in no uncertain terms I would fail graduation if I didn't do it. Pammie had already passed her test of faith by being told to jump off an 80 ft cliff head first, with no safety harness of any description. She did it, she passed and I had to pass my test to join her through to Righteous Class. She passed the test of faith that our new bodies were indestructible; only God knew how to erase that status; only God knew it's only weakness that would lead to eternal death if necessary and falling from 80 ft head first was not one of them and Pammie proved by faith that was so. She didn't even get a headache; it was like she had landed on a pile of cushions from just a foot high. I was so proud of Pammie but I was now faced with my test. I picked up the glass containing the hydrochloric acid and it felt so hot I didn't know if I could do it. The intensity of the hissing and the foaming coming from the glass was tormenting me to my very soul when I felt compelled to pray to God for help in finding my courage. By that very humble act I indeed was given help in finding my courage and picked up the glass of hydrochloric acid and poured it into my mouth ready to gulp it down as quickly as I could. It was like the most terrifying Bushtucker Trial in 'I'm a Celebrity' and to my amazement It was like drinking a chocolate milkshake. I had shown ultimate faith in ignoring what was presenting itself in front of me and gone ahead with my act of faith. I had also shown I wasn't too big to admit to God I needed his help; I humbled myself and that was such an important admission. I passed the final test, I had got that gold standard of faith and I was approved for baptism," said dad very proudly.

"Oh, my goodness, that is amazing," I shouted. "You were so brave and so incredibly clever. I hope I can be like you."

"They were trying to show that there have been so many people in the Bible that had to show faith to survive. It was the ultimate test of trust. Do you trust God? That was the crux of it all. Noah had to build an Ark to avoid drowning like the rest of mankind. He had to build an Ark when everyone was laughing at him and his family. He showed faith in God, he showed trust in God and no-one was laughing when the flood came were they? Daniel got thrown to the lions but wasn't hurt, the Israelites crossed the Red Sea and the waves parted for them to do so. They didn't falter thinking the waves would return. They trusted God in what was being told to them. It is daunting but I have every hope you will pass your very own test when the time comes," encouraged dad.

"I certainly hope so," I agreed, although everything dad had told me was making me sweat with nerves. I had certainly forgotten for a short time my angst over seeing my son with Amy Jane, I was going to have bigger fish to fry in the coming weeks and months.

"Would you like to stay at mine for the next few days?" asked dad. "You are given a little time to settle in this New Order before you start work as a cultivator and go to Theocratic School. I suggest you make the most of it."

"Yes, that would be fantastic. That is very nice of you," I replied.

"I've got a day off tomorrow. I would like to experience it with you," said dad.

"That would be great," I replied. "A game of tennis or a round of golf would be amazing. You are a fit young man now so it's anybody's guess who would win. It will be an amazing experience doing something with you."

"You are right, son," said dad. "But we are in the New Order now; there are no golf courses, but I can think of something even more amazing and spellbinding for you to consider."

"What's that, dad?" I asked.

"I thought a swim in the Mediterranean Sea, just off Gibraltar with a group of dolphins," suggested dad. "Wouldn't that be great?"

"That sounds wonderful," I replied. "But isn't that a long way to go?"

"It will be a first test for the power of your mind, I will help you," offered dad. "Our brains are so brilliant now, they have so much power compared to our previous lives. We can do anything that is not beyond reason. When I get baptised and get into Righteous Class there will be even more potential of the brain unlocked as you get closer to godlike standards. It is exciting, isn't it? I can't wait for tomorrow to see the look on your face when you have used your mind and brain properly for the first time and see what it is really capable of."

"I can't wait," I said and I was excited as it was such an intriguing prospect to use my brain in a new way, but I would have been just as excited doing anything with my dad again as he was alive again and a new man again. Just spending any time with him was precious enough for me and as the next day arrived I couldn't wait for our adventure.

"Are you ready for this, son?" asked dad.

"I am ready" I confirmed.

"Here is a picture of Gibraltar with the Rock of Gibraltar in the distance with the glorious blue Mediterranean Sea in the foreground and dolphins are jumping out the sea. Just visualise yourself there; focus your mind on that. Imagine you are in that sea swimming alongside them, I will be with you. Concentrate intently on that picture, concentrate intently on the thought you are there and execute your will that you are there. You will be teleported by thought and thought alone to that place you have focused on in your mind. Are you ready to execute?" encouraged dad. "Hold my hand; I am with you. I am doing the same as you."

Almost instantaneously we were there. We were swimming in the Mediterranean Sea in and around a group of Dolphins with the Rock of Gibraltar clearly in view, It felt miraculous and a glorious feeling of newly found wonder filled my being with just one exception: I was swimming in the Mediterranean Sea okay but I still had my full set of clothes on whereas dad was wearing swimming attire. He couldn't help bursting out laughing.

"I'm sorry, son. I didn't mean to laugh at you but have just learnt your first lesson," he said. "I am so happy you have achieved a teleport, but you also need to realise where you are teleporting to and you overlooked that bit. It just shows the discipline needed when you are using the power of your mind and the preparation required, but this is not a problem; just fully concentrate and imagine yourself there in swimming gear and swimming gear alone and execute that thought and you will be in that swimming gear.".

"That's better," I said as I achieved my mind's focus.

"You're a natural, son," commented dad. "You are now ready to enjoy our experience."

"It is almost like being in a holodeck adventure in Star Trek, isn't it?" I commented. "But this is very real, it's really happening, isn't it?"

"Yes, son, this is real," affirmed dad. "We don't need science fiction or fantasy in this world. It is real, our brains really can make things happen, It is wondrous."

"It certainly is," I agreed as my dad and I enjoyed such a beautiful time together. We were so lost in the moment it was nearly forgotten that we had to get back. It was nearly 7 pm; we had been swimming with dolphins for hours and it was only minutes before the daily mandatory Thanksgiving service to God.

"Come on, son, we need to get back. It's Thanksgiving to God and it is forbidden to miss it. I am soon going to be moving into the Righteous Class so I won't be able to go to Thanksgiving with you in the future, so let this time be precious. I am almost sorry that there will be a separation between us but I am sure it will only be temporary," said dad.

"There does seem to be a divide between the Righteous Class and the Unrighteous Class," I said. "Is that healthy? I don't want to be separated from you or mum or my son."

"It is necessary," dad replied. "It's the way of things. The Righteous don't mix with the Unrighteous, they teach them instead. It will be so beautiful when everybody is at the same level and are all baptised. Family can mix under very special circumstances, such as a resurrection but it is not encouraged beyond that I'm afraid."

"It seems very harsh," I said.

"I thought so at first but it was drummed into me how it was so important to concentrate on achieving parity with the Righteous by imitating their obedience, humility and subservience to God. It was of the upmost importance there was no distractions. Family had to come second so as not to distract you from what was now important. Relationships between Unrighteous people had to be approved and vetted by the Elders to see they were not acting as a distraction to the greater picture. I was very worried about Tony the Hawk when I was finding an attraction to Pammie. He used to give the most piercing looks of displeasure and disdain at us and I thought there was no way he would tolerate our affection towards each other but he could see we respected the rules and that we were fully engaged in the teaching so he allowed our relationship to continue. It was murder not being able to kiss Pammie but if I had done, Tony the Hawk would have noticed it. Absolutely nothing got by him; he had the eyes of an eagle. If I had transgressed I would have been banned from seeing Pammie. I probably would have been transferred for stewardship under a different Elder and received serious counselling for my transgression. The Theocratic School is very serious stuff; please prepare yourself wisely. I hope what I've told you helps you, as I don't want to be separated from you for too long, nor does your mum, nor your son. We all love you and look forward to the time we are of the same level," said dad. "I am glad that it's a week before I get baptised now as I want to spend quality time with you while I still can."

"So do I, dad," I agreed. "How hard is it for the Righteous to refrain from seeing members of the Unrighteous outside of the teaching work? You must have split families and loved ones; it must be so hard."

"It is very hard for them, I guess," said dad. "I know I will find it hard but it is like being cruel to be kind. The Unrighteous ones have to earn the right to join them and it is extra motivation for them to succeed if relationships depend on it so that is the way it is. If lives ultimately depend on it, you want nothing to get in the way of the focus and drive needed. We all benefit in the end with God's blessing and total peace in our souls."

I had loved seeing my dad again. I loved seeing him so happy and at peace. He so deserved to be happy. I hadn't seen Pammie yet but was looking forward to seeing her at some point. It seemed so cruel that almost as soon as I had seen my dad again I couldn't just see him automatically in the short term nor could I just automatically see my mum or my son unless approval was granted. In my son's case, it might have been the best medicine, as the sight of him all loved up with my beautiful Amy Jane was such a tormenting thing to have to endure. In light of that, Theocratic School and the impending challenges it provides could have been a welcome respite for me, and all I needed now was to know who my overseeing Elder was. I really hoped it would be Ewan or Levi, but it wasn't to be; I was getting Jefferson!

Just how hard was my life going to get?, Could I adapt to his harsh and brutal stewardship?, Could I find any ray of light? Or was my life in the New Order doomed to perpetual misery?.

As I prepared to get ready for my time at Theocratic School, having had the most wonderful and precious time with my dad, I was going to get another shock, as I lay in my bed half asleep, troubled with some trepidation at how I would get on at Theocratic School now I knew I had Jefferson as my guiding Elder, I could hear a voice; where was it coming from? It sounded like Amy Jane, but surely I was imagining it as Amy Jane would have been with Dean, and I only had dad for company. Everything went quiet again and I thought I must have be dreaming. When it started again, I definitely wasn't dreaming.

"Paul ….., Paul ….., can you hear me?" said the voice.

"Amy Jane? Is that you?" I replied.

"Yes Paul it is, do you want to talk?" said Amy Jane. "Don't be alarmed, you're hearing my thoughts. I am directing them to you. We can communicate by thought, It is so fantastic. Just concentrate your thoughts back on to me and I will receive them if it is what you wish."

"Where are you, Amy Jane?" I said.

"I'm at home with Dean. Don't worry, he is okay. He knows I wanted to clear the air with you. He can't hear this private communication but he trusts me. We can channel our thoughts and block them to other people if we need to. It's a bit like how you could block a person on Facebook in the old system. There is only God that it is impossible to block from your thoughts from." said Amy Jane. "So how are you? Have you started to get used to the New Order?"

"I am starting to adapt," I replied. "But I have to admit it was a great shock seeing you with my son. I love my son but I was gutted to see you with him. It made you unobtainable even if there wasn't these extra reimposed commandments to adhere to. I am having to get used to you never being my girl again and it hurts, It hurts so much but I know I have to move on and I will. I loved you so much and was even going to ask you to marry me on that very day I died. I had bought you such a beautiful ring and had arranged the most stunning bouquet of flowers to give you that evening."

"I'm so sorry I never got to be your wife," said Amy Jane. "I loved you very much as well. I would have said yes to you without hesitation. I guess we were never meant to be were we?. I am very happy with Dean but I do wonder what it would have been like to be your wife. I thought you were on the verge of asking me to be your wife; I could see in the way you looked at me just how much you loved me and I loved you just as much. I was absolutely devastated when you got killed. I cried my eyes out for months, I was inconsolable but eventually I had to move on. It went badly as no-one came close to how I felt for you until Dean came to my rescue. He reminded me so much of you; my feelings for him just got stronger and stronger until we decided to marry. There was never any guarantee I would ever see you again so it felt the right decision and still does as your son is a very good man but I can't help feeling what if?".

"It has been lovely to hear from you," I said. "It has really helped put the record straight. I can move on more easily from now on as it has set me at ease although I will find it so hard to find a girl as special as you. I start Theocratic School soon, so hearing from you has given me a major boost."

"It is lovely to hear that," replied Amy Jane. "Although unfortunately this has to be a one-off as it is not really becoming to be in 1:1 contact with a former love when I am a married lady even if you are now my father-in-law. You are family now to me."

"I hadn't thought of that," I replied. "Oh, my goodness, you are my daughter-in-law now. That feels so weird."

"It certainly does," agreed Amy Jane. "It feels surreal, doesn't it?. Who is your guiding Elder at Theocratic School?. I hope it's Ewan or Levi as I really hope you can become Righteous just like us as soon as possible. It's what we all want so much."

"It is Jefferson; my guiding Elder is Jefferson," I answered.

"Oh," said Amy Jane suddenly going very quiet as if she was trying very hard to hide her anguish.

"You're very quiet," I said. "You've gone quiet all of a sudden. Are you alright?"

"Yes, but I do think you have been given the most demanding guiding Elder," she replied. "They say Jefferson is remorseless, they say he is unyielding, they say he is relentless. I hope you will be okay. I will say a prayer for you."

"Thank you, Amy Jane, I hope I don't need prayers to help me. I am going to sleep now as it sounds like I need all the energy I can get if Jefferson is as described.

Hopefully I can knuckle down and achieve Righteous status as quick as I can," I said.

I was so glad to hear from Amy Jane but it had crystallised the realisation I had to move on, I had to try and find myself again, as the person I held so dear had moved on without me and I had to do the same. I was very nervous now about Theocratic School after what Amy Jane had said, but I couldn't change who I was given. Just how would the future pan out?

CHAPTER 5

A NEW LOVE

The year 0006 G.K.E (God's Kingdom era)

It was now coming up to a year at Theocratic School and all the warnings I had received about life under Jefferson's tutelage and guidance had unfortunately been proved correct. It had become an exhausting totalitarian and relentless regime, and there had been many times I had actually yearned to be put at peaceful rest once again, as it was seeming I was losing the will to live with the ferocity and unyielding nature of Jefferson's stewardship. I looked on with jealousy at how the other groups were given time to have valuable leisure time amongst their diligent studies. It seemed they had an ideal balance but not so in my case. It felt bleak and my morale was at an all time low in the New Order.

It wasn't that Jefferson was a bad man; it was far from it, but it was all two hundred miles an hour with him and no rest. How I yearned to be able to have downtime to discover more of myself and my new abilities.

In hindsight, Jefferson's unsquashable passion had helped me more than I realised, so I ought to have been grateful as the ability to endure under duress was a real sign of my perfection being tested, and having kept going under Jefferson's remorseless and unscrupulous supervision, it had cemented the long-suffering gold standard in the fruits of the spirit that I needed. I had made good progress after six months despite everything but I really didn't think I could stand another prolonged period under Jefferson.

It was during my darkest moments I spotted her, I spotted the girl who would change my life. I spotted the girl who would change my existence in the New Order. I spotted the girl who would finally make me forget about Amy Jane. Her name was Laura and she had only recently joined my group. She stood out immediately as there was something very different about her. She was very pretty with her long auburn hair; she was so gloriously feminine. I loved the way she giggled and acted with such free abandon. Laura had such a free spirit, I could not take my eyes off her. Her persona was magnetising, her allure was immense. I was instantly smitten as I could feel the butterflies in my stomach churning madly inside me. Everything about her was magical; I loved her eyes, I loved the way she coloured her nails, I loved her slimline figure. There was nothing I didn't like about her. I really wanted to get to know her but I was so wary of how Jefferson would perceive this if my concentration on theocratic studies was at all affected. I had to tread very carefully and pick my moment to engage. I so wanted her to like me and I thought my chance would never come as Bible study followed Bible study but then out of the blue and totally out of character Jefferson allowed a time out. I was pleasantly staggered but determined to make the most of it, I had to grab my chance of happiness; it might have been my only chance I thought as I nervously approached Laura.

"Hello, Laura, my name is Paul. How are you?" I stuttered.

"I'm fine, thank you," she replied. "And you?"

"I am great thanks. I really wanted to talk to you as I have noticed you have just arrived here. I wanted to be a friendly face as it can be overwhelming at first can't it?" I said.

"Yes, it is," agreed Laura. "I can't believe I am here in this New Order as it only seems like yesterday I was alive in a different world."

"Me too," I responded. "I actually died in a car accident on the 30th September 2000, so I was reborn into this world. I couldn't believe my eyes as my mum and dad were young again. It's unbelievable, isn't it?"

"I am sorry you were killed," said Laura. "I was, too."

"How did you die, Laura, if you don't mind me asking?"

"I drowned in a river accident," replied Laura. "It was on the 16th November 2000, just 2 months after you got killed."

"That's horrible. I know you might not want to talk about it, but how did that happen?" I asked.

"It was a very beautiful and crisp autumnal day. We had endured seemingly weeks of wet weather and I was eager to take advantage of that beautiful day with my boyfriend. We loved this romantic spot on a tree whose sturdy branches spread out over the River Thames below. We loved to kiss and cuddle and nestle up together there, It was our special place. I was enjoying the moment being stuck in his arms and all this turned to a bit of horseplay between us when I lost my balance, as my part of this thick branch suddenly snapped without warning. I fell in the river below, hitting my head on another heavy branch on the way down. I was knocked completely unconscious. The next thing I know I was waking up here, completely dazed and confused, not knowing where I was but surrounded by excited strangers I didn't know," revealed Laura. "I wanted to cry and I did."

"Didn't your family come and greet you, Laura?" I asked. "They did for me."

"I had no family waiting for me," answered Laura. "I was devastated to discover they hadn't made it. I cried even more when I realised the sad truth."

"What about your boyfriend? Didn't he make it?" I asked her.

"No, he didn't make it here either," she said sadly. "I don't know why as he seemed lovely. I would guess he was devastated at my death, particularly as he couldn't swim so he couldn't help me until it was too late. I am guessing that would have eaten him up and he probably had trouble coping with my loss."

"I am so sorry," I remarked. "We have some valuable downtime now. I was going to spend time with my family but I am willing to spend it with you if you want. It looks like you need a new friend to help support you. We all want the same thing, don't we, to make progress in this world. Everybody needs someone however perfect we are becoming."

"I guess so," answered Laura. Her enthusiasm for this New Order was not as strong as I imagined it would be but if you had lost all your family I guess it would have tainted it somewhat.

"I am not asking to be your boyfriend; we have only just met, but I won't lie to you – I find you attractive. I am drawn to you but I respect you as well. It might be too much for you to spend some free time together with me but I hope you say yes. I would be so happy to help you acclimatise to this world as Jefferson is so scary with his intensity isn't he?".

"I don't like him," revealed Laura, her revelation completely wrong-footing me.

"Why don't you like him, Laura?" I asked. "I know he's hard to cope with but he means well. We are supposed to love everybody in this world and to not judge others too harshly as God does the judging alone. I will try to help you see the good in him as the quality of love is such an important fruit of the spirit to get a gold standard in and you can't get it if you dislike a certain person. I hold my hands up; Jefferson is a big challenge but you can get over it if you really want it. I hope you can as your very progress is at stake and I want you to achieve Righteous status just like I want to."

"I appreciate what you are saying, Paul, It shows you care," replied Laura. "I will try harder but there is something you don't know about me."

"What's that?" I asked her.

"I was a very passionate feminist," revealed Laura. "I believed very strongly in women's rights. I lived in a very patriarchal world and I don't see this world as any different. It seems like men have more power than ever in this New Order; they make all the decisions. I haven't noticed one woman in authority. I am very troubled by this. I did have a boyfriend but I do have a very big mistrust of men. I am a girl's girl and I loved my girly mates but I haven't met any girl in this New Order with my sense of fun. It all seems very supressed. I don't know if I can get used to this New Order; I don't know if I want to."

"Please don't say that, Laura," I implored her. "You're lovely; I will be your champion." It suddenly dawned on me I was instantly falling for her. I was amazed at my chagrin at hearing Laura wasn't totally happy here; it was a sign she had an instant hold over me.

"You are saying some lovely things, Paul. It is lovely that you care and that you like me," said Laura. "I am willing to spend some free time with you. I would usually only want to spend time with the girls but they are no fun here, so yes, I can feel I would be okay with you."

"I am so happy you've said that," I said. "I know you are frustrated with certain things but what about the amazing things that can be done in this new world?, The bond between us and the animals? Our perfect bodies, our perfect minds and being able to teleport, Have you teleported yet?"

"No, I didn't realise I could," revealed Laura.

"Nobody's told you?" I asked her, feeling aghast. "It is wonderful what our minds can now do. What about communicating by thought and thought alone?"

"No, nobody has told me about that, either," said Laura.

"I will help you," I said. "It might change how you see this world. It is an awesome ability we have now been given. Would you like to have an adventure with me?"

"Yes, I am excited, Paul," enthused Laura. "Let's do it!"

"What have you always wanted to do, Laura?" I asked her. "Think of something special you have always wanted to experience."

"I would love to see the gorillas in the mist," answered Laura. "I would love to go to the Rwandan jungle and see the gorillas in their natural habitat, a nice happy family of gorillas. I love animals."

"Let's go there right now," I encouraged her.

"What do I have to do?" asked an excited Laura.

"Focus intently on the jungle with the gorillas in it, focus intently on that image in your mind. Focus on your attire and execute that thought. I will do the same. Let our thoughts mingle as we lock on together to that image. It will become reality, we will be in the image," I encouraged her.

"I am nervous; I haven't done this before. Promise you will be with me, Paul," said Laura.

"Of course I will, Laura," I replied comforting her. "Don't be nervous, you'll love it."

"Okay, here goes, then," said Laura as she opened the floodgates of her mind to see herself amongst the jungle habitat of Rwanda with a family group of gorillas joyfully playing together. There was a very cute baby gorilla being cradled by its mother and they were not scared or anxious of Laura's presence, they were at peace with her. It was beautiful to see and as Laura turned around to see my comforting presence she couldn't help getting very emotional.

"This is amazing, the gorillas are amazing. I am so overwhelmed," she cried with such joyful tears of wonder. "The baby gorilla is so cute I want to hug it."

"Go on then, Laura, you can," I urged her. "They are not scared of you. The mommy gorilla trusts you; she will let you hug her baby and the baby gorilla will not be in distress."

"Are you sure, Paul, Are you really sure?" asked Laura, trying so hard to contain her doubts.

"I am positively sure Laura. No animals will ever hurt humans now and vice versa. It is the new way of things," I encouraged her, completely putting her at ease.

"Oh my god, he is lovely," said Laura as she happily cradled the baby gorilla. "And the mum is letting me do it. This is so beautiful."

"I am going to let the daddy gorilla take me for a ride on his back. I will be back soon," I replied. "We are going for a swing amongst the trees. This is going to be such a thrill."

"Be careful, Paul," said Laura.

"Don't worry, there is no danger anymore but I will be careful. I will be back soon and then we need to return back to Theocratic School," I answered.

"Okay," said Laura, who by now was radiating happiness and contentment. She was a revitalised person and I was so happy I was the person who had enabled this.

"Thank you, Paul, for a most wonderful date," she enthused.

"I am so glad you are calling it a date," I replied. "Does this mean we can do something like this again together?"

"Absolutely," encouraged Laura. "I really enjoyed having an adventure with you today. Thank you, Paul, you have been so nice; you really know how to make a girl happy."

This was just the start of a new and beautiful blossoming relationship and I couldn't have been happier. As the months followed, we both made good progress at Theocratic School, propelled by massive springs in our step. We had gone on further adventures like surfing on Bondi Beach, Australia, and a safari in South Africa. It looked like I had melted an ice maiden and charmed her into being my proper girlfriend as she finally let me hold her hand.

"You do know what this means, don't you, Laura?"

"Yes, I do," she replied.

"In this world it is like a solemn vow. Holding hands is saying you are one with me. We are an item; we are committed to each other now. Are you sure you want to do it, Laura?" I asked her. "Because I really want to be able to hold your hand. I know it means an intention to marry you; it is akin to a marriage proposal, isn't it, in this world, but I love you, Laura. I think you're so pretty. You are a special girl."

"I am happy to be your girlfriend and more than happy for us to be holding hands," replied Laura. "I am fully aware what it represents, a special commitment between two people. You have already shown me enough for me to know that you are the right person for me. You've shown me such love and respect, I realise you are the one. I am a lucky girl."

"It is me that is the lucky one," I countered.

"There is only one thing wrong," said Laura.

"What's that?" I asked.

"I want to snog the face off you," she said. "I want to get my hands on you. It is so frustrating we can't."

"You're not kidding, it is incredibly frustrating," I agreed. "I so look forward to when we can seal our passion. I am so looking forward to showing you off to my family. They will be so happy for me. They will be family to you from now on."

"I am so happy, Paul," cried Laura.

I had met the girl that had rocked my new world; I had met the girl who could and would change my life. I had met the girl who was the welcome antidote to the pain of losing Amy Jane to my son. I had met the girl I was going to marry and live forever with. I had discovered utopia but was utopia about to be snatched from me? Trouble brewed on the horizon as I was about to discover you can't always get what you want. Was I on my way to another heartbreak?

CHAPTER 6

TROUBLE IN PARADISE

It had been the most exhilarating period of my life as I enjoyed my electric romance with Laura. I had even embraced the rabid teachings of Jefferson. The end was in sight to my Theocratic School existence as I prepared for my final test, the test of faith. In truth, I really wasn't looking forward to the test of faith as my dad described his test as extremely challenging but he passed it and so could I. I wondered with dread what my test would entail as with Jefferson in charge it had to be extremely unpleasant I thought. I couldn't have been more wrong and I should have smelled a rat!

Being able to finally call myself Righteous Class should have been my gateway to everlasting happiness. The only trouble was Laura was a good two months away at current progress of achieving similar status. There would need to be a great divide between us for a short period of time as Righteous people were not encouraged to mix with Unrighteous people, but I thought, with some justification, that Laura would be an exception. As our relationship was pure and true, wasn't it cruel if we were denied each other's company? We had obeyed all the rules, we had shown respect for the New Order, we had done this despite enormous mutual arousal. Holding hands seemed so grossly inadequate when two people were in love. In the heightened electrical confines of our relationship, it had taken every last reserve of mental discipline in our perfecting minds to resist our natural urges that our romance became highly physical and passionate but we had shown admirable resistance in the circumstances. What we wanted now was understanding; surely that was not too much to ask, but it was!.

I should have realised something was up when I proudly showed off my new girlfriend, Laura, to my family. It wasn't the reaction I was expecting; it was muted rather than euphoric. I hadn't yet taken my final test of faith and it was the first time I began to wonder if joining the Righteous Class was as life-affirming as I thought it would be. I was almost hoping I would fail my test and it would buy me and Laura more time together. To think I was so excited as Laura and I arrived at mum's palatial home. I was going to be sorely disappointed!

"Hello, mum, I would like you to meet Laura. I've asked her to be my wife in this new system. We have already held hands but I am sure she is the one for me. She makes me very happy," I said, waxing lyrical about how Laura made me feel.

"That's ....., that's ....., er, great, Paul," answered mum in an extremely unconvincing and underwhelming manner, leaving me perplexed and a little irritated at her lack of enthusiasm. What was her problem? Surely she was happy for me, wasn't she? I was beginning to regret coming, as I was invited into their vast living room where Dean and Amy Jane were waiting to greet us. I was pleased that Dean was rather more cheery.

"Well done, dad. I am really happy for you. I am so glad you have met a nice girl. It is nice to meet you, Laura," he said, with heartfelt empathy, obviously feeling that now I had found love, it was a monkey off his back as he was married to Amy Jane whom I had previously loved so dearly. Amy Jane was rather less overjoyed, it seemed, than Dean was.

"Yes, I am glad for you as well. I am sure Laura will make you happy," she commented. It was the tone in which she said it that was far from convincing me it was meant in the right spirit. Surely her tone wasn't betraying her real feelings, was it? Could I even detect a little bit of jealousy? If I didn't know better, Amy Jane sounded a little bitchy.

"So how did you meet?" asked Dean. "Was it at Theocratic School?"

"Yes. I noticed Laura straight away and immediately knew she was the one for me. When you meet someone special, you immediately know, don't you?" I said.

"You're making me blush, Paul," protested Laura as she tried to play down how attractive she was. Laura was never the best at taking compliments as she had learned this only usually came from disingenuous males out for what they could get. She had learned how to grow a thick skin out of her suspicion of the male sex. It had hardened her feminist drive which made it harder for her to accept compliments.

"Were you resurrected like my dad then, Laura?" asked Dean.

"Yes, I was. I drowned in a tragic accident," she answered. "I guess that's why I have been given a second chance of life."

"I am glad you have had another chance," said Dean.

"What did you do in your previous life?" asked Amy Jane, who was finally involving herself in the conversation.

"I was a nurse, an intensive care nurse," answered Laura.

"Oh, that's, er ....., er, quaint." Replied Amy Jane.

"I think it's a very laudable profession," interrupted Dean.

"But one that has become obsolete, hasn't it?" argued Amy Jane, almost mocking its past the sell by date usefulness. "It is of no use now, is it? Do you think you could become a good teacher? That is what is really important," she added scornfully.

"I am sure I could be if I wanted to be; no doubt at all," scoffed Laura, clearly sensing a sisterly lack of warmth coming from Amy Jane.

"If? ....., If? ...... That's an interesting choice of word, don't you think? You should have said 'when'. You are expressing doubt and a lack of clarity or certainty," admonished Amy Jane.

"I think this is starting to feel a little awkward," I said wanting to put a lid on things. I noticed mum had said very little up to this point. "You're very quiet, mum. What's on your mind?"

"Nothing, Paul," she said.

I could tell when she was lying and this disturbed me very much because lying was not becoming of a member of the Righteous Class. God hated liars so perhaps I was mistaken, but I had a strong sense she was hiding something from me. I didn't want to push her further at this point but something was not right. What was she not telling me? The rest of my family meeting with Laura couldn't end quick enough for me but mum did leave a very cryptic farewell message on our way out.

"Good luck, Paul, with your test of faith. I can't wait for you to succeed and join us in the Righteous Class. Things will be so different; I can't wait for the transformation when you pass."

I was very perturbed, as what did she mean by 'transformation'? I didn't want things to be different. My mum also said when I pass, not if I pass; it could have been a massive vote of confidence in me, but it was the perceived certainty of the way she implied it which really unnerved me. The test of faith was like taking a driving test in the old system; it was by no means certain you would pass first time. I had seen countless students fail in my short time at Theocratic School and they had to start all over again, so why was mum so sure I would pass?. It was like it was already a given.

The test of faith was no picnic, no picnic at all. It required supreme courage married to supreme faith. It wasn't called a gold standard test of faith for no reason. Why was mum so confident in me?

I was soon going to find out in my moment of truth, my moment of divine truth. Jefferson had shortlisted a dozen people for the test of faith and I was the last of them. Laura watched on as I prepared; I could see her eyes misting up with worry. She gazed lovingly towards me as I disappeared from view. If I passed, I didn't realise the ramifications for our relationship at that point in time; I knew Laura would soon face and pass her own test, reuniting us in Righteousness, so it hadn't occurred to me I was on the point of no return concerning Laura.

Jefferson seemed to take great delight in showing me and the other shortlisted students that we were going to be bitten by a black mamba snake whose poison could be extremely toxic and deadly, leading to excruciating paralysis and death within a very short time, but of course we had to show faith this wouldn't happen. Five of the first ten students couldn't go through with it which I didn't know as we were all separate and individual from each other. We didn't know how each other was doing so as not to affect our own judgment. I won't lie, I was sweating profusely; I was not looking forward to this and I didn't want to go through with it. Every fibre in my being was telling me to pull out and that passing this very unpleasant test would see me becoming unhappier, not happier. A poisonous black mamba was very scary so there was no dishonour in failing my first test; there would be other chances. I was preparing my excuses when Jefferson called me in. Where was the black mamba? It wasn't there!

"Where's the snake?" I asked Jefferson. "I thought I was going to get bitten by one to prove my faith. I was going to tell you I can't do it."

"There is no snake for you to be tested," disclosed Jefferson. "That was for the others. You have a different test."

"What's that?" I asked, gulping with fear to what Jefferson had planned for me.

"It's over there," Jefferson pointed. "You are going to get bitten by that creature; this is your ultimate test of faith and if you let it bite you then you have passed the course and you will receive your baptism into the Righteous Class."

"I can only see your pet Yorkshire terrier. That isn't a true test of faith, is it?" I said, incredulously.

"It is for you," said Jefferson.

"I feel like a fraud; this can't be right," I protested. "I was preparing for the snake; I was preparing my excuses."

"I know," said Jefferson. "That is why there is now no excuse for you to avoid this test. I want you passed and out of here. You have no choice; if you refused to be bitten by a Yorkshire terrier you would be a laughing stock, a figure of ridicule. You have no excuses do you?.

"But why are you making this too easy for me?, I asked. "This does not feel right at all; this does not feel sincere or honourable. Why are you doing this to me?.

"I don't have to tell you," said Jefferson, "but all I will say is ask your mum and all will be revealed."

I was snookered; I had nowhere to hide, nowhere to run. I had to let his Yorkshire terrier bite me and it was just a pathetic little nip that, of course, left no pain. That was my test of faith and I felt terrible. I felt no sense of accomplishment at all. I felt a rotten emptiness inside and as I prepared to leave and tell Laura all about it, Jefferson had another blow to my stomach to give me.

"Where do you think you're going?" he said.

"I am going to see Laura and tell her the news," I replied, feeling so deflated.

"I am afraid you can't see Laura," was Jefferson's dismissive reply.

"Why not? She is my girlfriend; I want to see her," I protested.

"You can't. She is Unrighteous. It is now forbidden for you to see her unless you were her teacher, which you're not. You are a Righteous person in waiting now; you can't mix with her anymore."

"This is ridiculous. Laura is my girlfriend; I love her and I want to be with her," I shouted.

"I am afraid that is not possible," warned Jefferson. "If you transgress, you will be in violation of the rules of the New Order. You will be thrown out to a certain second death. Do you understand?"

"This is not right, I am not happy!" I said, angrily.

"I know you are trying to provoke me with your emotions," said Jefferson. "Anger is not becoming of the Righteous Class but your anger won't last. Your baptism will see you enhanced in the perfection process; your anger will reside and fade. It won't exist once you are conditioned."

"Conditioned?, What do you mean, conditioned?" I asked, feeling great apprehension.

"You will be conditioned to a life lived in true peace and harmony," declared Jefferson. "All unnecessary emotions will be removed from you. You will comply".

"I still don't understand why this is happening and how I have passed so easily," I argued. "I love Laura; she will become Righteous in time. Why does it seem like you want to deprive me and her of our love when it is only a matter of a few weeks?"

"Like I said, ask your mum," said Jefferson. "All I will say is, don't take it for granted Laura will join you in the Righteous Class. Don't believe it is inevitable, it isn't. I think the quicker you can move on without her the better. That is my advice."

"I think I will pass over your advice," I declared defiantly, although I was now greatly troubled at how Jefferson had cast doubt on Laura's progress. Jefferson had the power to maintain the chasm that now existed between myself and Laura. I was furious and I wanted answers fast. It seemed mum did know something I didn't; what was it?

Before I saw my mum again I wanted to catch up with dad, It had been ages since I last saw him. How was he? He had gone before me in managing to get into the Righteous Class from the Unrighteous underclass. He had met a new girl in Pammie; I still hadn't met her as I had been so busy. There was so much to catch up on and I hoped dad could enlighten me and prepare me for what to come. I looked up to him so much; he was my inspiration, my template. If anybody knew what I was going through, it was dad and as I prepared to call on him, I was in for my first shock; his modest but homely dwelling had gone and been upgraded to a much more palatial abode.

"Wow! Dad, this is quite a change, isn't it? This place is so big now and so modern and you have an expansive garden. Is this all because you are now Righteous?"

"Yes, son. Do come in and have a good look around," encouraged dad. "It takes some getting used to, doesn't it, The last time I saw you it was basically a glorified hut; you couldn't swing a cat, could you, in here?

Pammie will be coming round soon; she is so excited to meet you. I am so happy she is now my wife ".

"Congratulations, dad, you deserve it," I replied. "I am glad someone is happy."

"Aren't you happy, son?" said dad. "I heard you have passed the Theocratic course so I thought you would be very pleased with yourself, but you look like you have the weight of the world on your shoulders. What's up, Paul?"

"I am very troubled, dad. Something is very wrong," I replied. "I should be very happy but I am not. I met this lovely girl called Laura and we had even held hands. She is the girl I wanted to marry in this New Order now Amy Jane was never going to be mine. Everything had been set up, and yet by passing through to Righteous Class, it means I can't see her anymore, and Jefferson even intimated it could be for a very long time. I feel so deflated; I have no elation whatsoever, I feel bereft. This is not how it's supposed to be, is it? Please tell me it isn't, dad."

"I haven't had any problems, son," answered dad. "Me and Pammie passed on the same day. We are one and I am so happy. Pammie's here, she would like to say hello to you."

"Hello, Paul, it is so good to meet you. I have heard a lot about you as your dad is very proud of you," she said.

I turned round to greet her and was then stunned into silence. Pammie was an absolute blonde bombshell. She looked like Pamela Anderson from Baywatch; surely it wasn't really her, was it? Her name was Pammie, after all, and she could be her doppelganger.

"Your surname isn't Anderson, is it, by any chance?" I asked her.

"Yes, it is," answered Pammie.

"You're not THE Pammie Anderson, are you? You look just like her, the girl from Baywatch."

"I will keep you guessing on that one," teased Pammie.

"Dad, you have played a blinder; you know I think you're great but I have to say you are batting above your average there. I can't believe you have met such a stunning lady. No wonder you are so happy and I am so happy for you. They do say good things happen to good people and it certainly has been in your case, hasn't it?"

"Absolutely," agreed dad. "I am more than alright. I am so sorry you have problems. I do think I have an inkling what is going on and I do not think it's right, if I am being honest."

"I don't like the sound of that," I said. "What do you think is going on?"

"It sounds like you have been chosen for an arranged marriage, that is what I suspect. I think someone already in the Righteous Class has earmarked you to join another person. I have heard it happens quite regularly," revealed dad. "I wonder who they have got lined up for you?"

"I hope you are wrong, dad. This is not right, this is a nightmare," I said, feeling extremely outraged. "Jefferson told me to ask mum; she knows something. I am going to ask her what the hell is going on. I am not happy; I have already met my dream girl. Marriage is supposed to be sacrosanct, isn't it, especially in this world. Marriage is supposed to be between two people that are perfectly suited to each other who love each other. Now I am being led to believe it can be manipulated to serve other purposes. This is not right!"

"I agree with you son if it's any consolation," said dad. "Go and see your mum and find out what she can tell you. Before you go, I do want to warn you about one thing, though son, and it's about your forthcoming baptism at the Righteous Class convention."

"What's that, dad?" I asked him, hardly wanting to be given another nasty shock.

"Everybody will be naked," he warned. "I will be naked, Pammie will be naked, your mum will be naked, your son Dean and his wife Amy Jane will be naked. All the Elders will be naked as well as all of the Righteous class at this convention. In fact, everybody is going to be naked except you. You will be clothed when you arrive at the convention, but once you are baptised you will be naked also."

"What?" I shrieked. "This is a nightmare to end all nightmares. Me naked in front of everybody; you and mum and all my family naked as well? I don't think I can do this; I don't think I want to do this. Why is this so necessary?."

"It is all about the stripping of the old personality. It is symbolic," answered dad. "You have got rid of all the imperfection and the clothes represent the imperfection. You have no choice, son. I didn't want to do it but I had no choice. When God created the first humans, Adam and Eve, they were perfectly happy being naked. They didn't even notice they were naked. It was a sign of their perfection that they were so comfortable with how they were and it was only when they were disobedient they realised they were naked. So, the fact all the Righteous are naked when they are together is their proof of perfection. They are being aligned with how the original Adam and Eve were made. It will be the eternal way of things in the New Order once all the Unrighteous have passed into the Righteous Class. Everybody will be naked; nobody will bat an eyelid. We will all be in a different state of existence by then."

"Wow!" Was all I could say as I stood there open-mouthed. I was now supposed to be comfortable being naked and seeing all my loved ones naked from now on. I was supposed to be comfortable seeing Jefferson and his fellow Elders naked. I wasn't comfortable with that. I wasn't supposed to feel vulnerable with everybody staring at me; I wasn't supposed to be self-conscious anymore but I still felt self-conscious despite getting through Theocratic School. For the first time in my second life in this New Order I felt alone, I felt vulnerable; I even felt scared as I was now having trouble fitting in. I was starting to feel I didn't belong in this New Order. I was very troubled in this paradise. How I yearned for the innocence of the Unrighteous where I was so happy with Laura and completely oblivious to what was to come. Being flawed and imperfect did not seem to be the worst thing in the world and I was missing it now.

I yearned for watching the Villa; there was no Villa in the New Order. I yearned for pop concerts; there were no pop concerts in the New Order. I yearned for all my favourite television programmes; there was no television in the New Order. It was now I realised what had been lost to me in this New Order. I enjoyed my first life despite all its frailties. I did not know if I wanted to live forever in this paradise if I couldn't be me. I loved God, I wanted to be a good person but it didn't seem to be enough.

I had lost the sudden urge to confront mum as I felt all the wind had been taken from my sails, I was adrift on a sea of misery. This was not what perfection was supposed to be about. I didn't think anything mum said was going to pacify me the way I was feeling. It had been two weeks since I passed Theocratic School, two weeks since I last saw and spoke to Laura. I know I had been forbidden to contact her but with my baptism at the Righteous Convention only a day away I had to act now and act fast and to hell with the consequences. I had to contact Laura to see how she was, how she was coping without me at Theocratic School. Was she any nearer to getting her own pass into the Righteous Class? I could not bear not knowing how she was as I loved her.

So it was that very night I made the decision to contact with her in my mind as I was distraught of the thought at not seeing her. It was unbearable not to be her boyfriend and potential husband anymore. I was genuinely miserable, my morale at rock bottom. What is a life if you have so much restraint, it doesn't feel like a life anymore? I had to be me and if that wasn't good enough then C'est la vie.

I was so nervous as I locked onto Laura's mind, ready to use the communication of thought. I really didn't know how she would react but I had to find out for my own sanity.

"Laura ....., Laura ....., can you hear my thoughts?"

"Is that you, Paul?" she answered. "I've missed you so much. How are you doing? It is not fair I can't see you anymore. I so want to see you; I want to be able to hold you again and feel your love for me.

"I want that too, desperately," I replied. "How are you getting on at Theocratic School? Please tell me you are doing well, as I want you to get Righteous Class status as quickly as possible. I want us to be together once again. I love you."

"I love you too, Paul," said Laura, whose sad voice implied something was wrong, something very wrong.

"What's up, Laura?" I asked her, feeling very concerned. "It sounds like you are on the verge of tears."

"I am sorry, Paul," replied Laura. "It's just ....., just ....."

"Just what, Laura? Please tell me; I am really worried," I urged.

"It's ….. Jefferson," replied Laura. "I think he has it in for me. It is like he doesn't want me to succeed and I don't know why."

"What's happened, Laura? What has he done?" I asked her, knowing full well there seemed to be ulterior motives at work. He had warned me of it, to all intents and purposes.

"A day after you left, he put me forward for a test of faith hoping I would fail it and have to start all over again. He wanted to delay my passage, I am sure of it knowing what I know now," revealed Laura.

"What did you have to do, Laura? What was your test of faith?" I asked her.

"I had to put my head inside the jaws of a saltwater crocodile, a fully grown saltwater crocodile. I was petrified, but Jefferson insisted I had to do it. I think he thought I wouldn't do it and pull out but us females are tough. I did it; I proved him wrong. I thought he would endorse my passage to Righteous Class as a result, but all he said was he couldn't put me through until I agreed with all the mantra of the New Order which I did, for the most part, as it was all good. But there was one major sticking point for me that he knew I had great trouble in accepting. Jefferson had found my weak point; he had me where he wanted me. I was not going to back down and as a result, I was refused acceptance for passage through to Righteous Class. Even worse, I have been told I have to start all over again for my perceived insolence. I am heartbroken, Paul. I really wanted you back in my arms again."

"What part of the mantra couldn't you subscribe to, Laura?" I asked her. "What was it hard for you to accept?"

"It was the Be in Subjection to Male Authority section," she answered. "In my previous life, I was very much a modern woman. I loved having feminine confidence and parading it. I loved my independent power. I did have a nice boyfriend but he respected me as you do. I found a lot of men had an insufferable ego; they thought they were better than us and for such a long time women like my mother, but especially my grandmother, were treated like second class citizens. Men were in charge and didn't we know about it. As a modern woman, I could see ladies rise to positions of power and influence to be alongside men and now I am having to accept it is almost like the world has gone full circle again and I don't like it. The women are in subjection all over again; it is almost like living in the 1950's again and I am part of it. Men have all the power again; all the Elders are men and some, like Jefferson, really have an arrogant strut about them. Jefferson has picked up on my difficulty accepting the subjection rules and has really started to press my buttons and my perfection, or growing perfection, hasn't managed to combat this. I am afraid now you are no longer around. The way he is treating me is really making me question whether I want to be here. I really don't know if this world is for me."

"Please don't say that, Laura," I begged. "We have perfect bodies; we have fantastic brain power. We don't suffer disease or aches and pains; we don't fall ill. The weather is perpetually beautiful and it is such paradise all around us with the animals now truly our best friends. Don't lose faith in it all, Laura."

It was a powerful advert I was giving to Laura but it was almost like I was trying to convince myself at the same time. It pained me to say it but it looked like we both had really found trouble in paradise.

CHAPTER 7

THE END OF THE BEGINNING (ALICE IS EXPECTING YOU!)

"What is going on, mum?" I implored her to answer. "I love you but you must tell me what is going on. I need answers; everything is not right. I am getting baptised later today and it is like I don't want to. Every instinct in my body is telling me to refrain and to not go. I really don't want to go, mum."

"You have to, Paul. You have no choice. If you don't go you will die," warned mum. "Whatever is the matter?"

"There is something you know that you are not telling me. I have been banned from seeing Laura whom I was in love with. I was given a ridiculously easy test of faith and when I asked Jefferson about it, he alluded you knew something. There is even a suspicion and talk of me having an arranged marriage in the pipeline. Is this true, mum?, How can that be fair? Is this right? as it seems to make a mockery of real love," I protested.

"Sit down, Paul. I don't know how you found out about this but it is true," confessed mum. "There is this girl called Alice and you have been betrothed to her. She is the daughter of an Elder. It will be the making of you as you pass into Righteousness. It will guarantee you living in splendour. A mum always wants what is best for her son and I am no different. Alice is a nice girl, so prim and proper and so Righteous. She is a highly regarded ministerial teacher. This is her picture by the way, I think you will be happy with her as your wife for eternity."

"Happy with her?" I shouted with incredulity. "I haven't even met the girl. She probably is a nice girl but she is not my Laura. How could anybody just presume I could just switch to another girl just like that? Riches and power and status doesn't buy happiness; I thought that lesson from our imperfect past had been learnt. It was supposed to be about being meek and humble to inherit this Earth (*Psalms 37.10 and 11*). I have to say, I am beginning to question this New Order's authenticity."

"You are being silly, Paul," said mum. "You are getting baptised later; you will get engaged to Alice. You will get used to it; you will comply."

I was seriously thinking about running away when mum warned, "It is not just about you; think of Laura. If you truly love her you will let her go. I am sure Laura's path will be made a lot easier if you comply, if you know what I mean.

I reluctantly made the decision to go ahead with my baptism, much to my chagrin. I couldn't bear thinking of how unhappy Laura sounded. I wanted her to be happy, I loved her. Everything seemed futile, resistance seemed futile. I would comply with a heavy heart and cross the Alice bridge when it came to it. Maybe she wouldn't want to be my girl for eternity. Maybe she would get me a get out of jail free card and end my nightmare. I lived in hope that that the shackles being put on Laura would end.

As I arrived at the Righteous Convention, I felt more like a condemned man rather than someone on the brink of eternal salvation. I looked up into the massed crowd and in the front row I winced as I could see my dad naked, my mum naked, dean and Amy Jane naked, my two nieces, Jodie and Lollypop and their husbands, Luke and Jonathan naked, my sister naked. I could see Ewan, Levi, Tony The Hawk and Jefferson naked. Everybody was naked and they were looking on expectantly. Alice, my prospective bride to be was also sitting there naked with them. What an introduction that was for me as I hadn't even said hello to her!.

The Convention started with a major announcement; a new scroll was being opened. What did it say? It said that from now on any couple could only have one child and this was finite. The act of sex was going to be completely outlawed in less than 100 years as it was then no longer necessary. God had built having sex into our DNA to facilitate reproduction and as reproduction was being phased out, so was sex. The Righteous cheered their recognition of the scroll but I was gutted, It was another pleasure to be put on the banned list. I was finding it hard to hide my misery.

The Convention continued to run on for hours when I was summoned to receive my baptism. It was time to take my clothes off and I felt so exposed, like at no other time in my life. My mum looked so proud and the others with her hadn't batted an eyelid; it was like they had seen it all before. I was as nervous as I had ever been. It was then I noticed how stern the atmosphere was. It was so serious; joy and laughter seemed to have left the building. There was an austerity of emotion all around. I didn't want to feel like this but it was too late. I was in the specially prepared pool and subsequently immersed in it, I was baptised; I was a member of the Righteous Class. It had been done.

My mum, my very proud mum, summoned me over as she proclaimed, "I am so proud of you, Paul. You have made my dreams come true."

"Yes, well done, son," said dad. "You are one of us now," as Pammie kissed me on the cheek in solidarity.

"Well done, dad. I am so glad you've joined us," declared Dean.

"Yes. Well done, Paul," said Amy Jane. "We can all be one whole happy family now."

"Say hello to Alice, Paul," encouraged mum. "She is here to offer her congratulations at her husband to be."

"Er ....., er ......, hello, Alice," was all I could muster.

"It is nice to see you, Paul," she said. "You were so good out there. I am delighted for you and so happy we will become one flesh."

"Er ….., er ….., steady on a bit," I replied. "I am happy to see you but I don't even know you yet. I have never even had a conversation with you and yet you are stood in front of me and we both have no clothes on."

"I know. It's great, isn't it?" said Alice. "We don't need clothes when we are amongst our Righteous selves. It is only when we mix with the Unrighteous, having to teach them. We will be so happy together naked."

"Er ….., er ….., I guess so," was all I could say as I contemplated my future with dread. I didn't even know the girl! I didn't know if we had anything in common and yet I was being yoked to her.

"Do you want to hold my hand, Paul?" asked Alice.

"Er ….., er ….., not just yet," I replied. "Let's go and speak together in a private place and get to know each other first. I am sure you want to find out more about me if we are to marry, don't you?"

"No, not really," said Alice. "You're mine; that's all I need to know".

"You might not like me," I replied, trying to make her see sense.

"I do like you," said Alice. "Do you like me?"

"You seem like a nice girl, but what do we have in common? What would we like to do together?" I asked her. "We need to discuss these things. Do you like teleporting? What or where would you like to go when you teleport?"

"I don't like teleporting," she answered. "It's boring."

"Boring?" I questioned Alice. "I love teleporting. I think that is one thing we already disagree on. It is not a good start."

"Teleporting is so unnecessary when you've got me," Alice replied. "I want a full-time ministerial partner and you're it; husband and wife forever indulged in the teaching work. Twenty hours a day is not unreasonable for us, is it? My motto is, all work and no play make a happy couple today. Do you feel the same as me, Paul?"

"Er ….., er ….., I hadn't thought of it like that," I replied, feeling tremendous trepidation at how Alice saw our union.

"You have heard there is no rest for the Righteous, haven't you, Paul? Well, there really is no rest for the Righteous. I want us to be the next Mark and Kelly, or Jodie and Jonathan. They are the star couples; I want us to emulate them," urged Alice.

"It is certainly something to strive for," I agreed, trying to placate her. "They are indeed star couples, aren't they?"

"Oh, Paul, you are making me such a happy girl," eulogised Alice. "Let's get married!"

"Er ....., er ....., let's just hang on just a little bit," I encouraged her, clearly regretting my faux pas in trying to play along with her. I had created a monster.

"But all the Righteous couples marry quickly," argued Alice. "They can't wait to marry. We should marry straightaway, just like them. I have been single too long. I want to be married just like the others. I love weddings; I go to one every week. It is about time I had my own wedding. I am desperate to be married, Aren't you?"

I was in big trouble as my life was spinning out of my control. I managed to talk Alice into waiting for a few weeks to marry. She was not happy as she said it was longer than all of the other couples but I was desperately trying to buy time in the hope Laura would come through somehow, but as time elapsed, it was obvious she wasn't coming through.

As my wedding day crept up on me with indecent speed, I was missing Laura more than ever. I couldn't live like this. Being Righteous was not the utopia I had been sold. It was like being in a world of Vulcans, where emotions were not welcome. My mind was made up; I was going to contact Laura again before it was too late. I couldn't go through with the marriage to Alice; it wasn't right or fair on either of us. Alice was not a bad girl; she was a sweet girl. She deserved to find happiness with someone that was truly suited to her and who loved her for who she was, and not have a person like me manufactured to do that. I was in love with another girl called Laura. Alice didn't deserve living a lie and that's what it was. I had to act for both our sakes and if that meant I had to suffer the consequences, then so be it.

It had been over three weeks since I last spoke to Laura as I nervously tuned into her with my thoughts.

"Laura ....., Laura ....., can you hear me?"

"Yes I can, Paul," replied Laura, "but won't you be in trouble? You shouldn't be contacting me. You are Righteous now and I am nowhere near achieving it. I am too rebellious to be accepted any time soon. You need to move on, Paul; forget about me."

"I don't want to forget about you, Laura. I never will. I never will give up on you," I argued. "I don't care if I get in trouble; you are worth it. As far as I am concerned, you are still my girlfriend."

"I can't be your girlfriend now, Paul, can I?" said Laura. "They have already told you that, haven't they?"

"They have said that," I confirmed "but I can't accept it. They want me to marry a Righteous girl called Alice but I want you; my heart belongs to you."

Laura started crying. "This is horrible. How can they be so insensitive? The way they want to write me out of your life and discard me is so cruel. It seems they want to take you away from me with indecent haste; I am so upset. God is love; this is not love. I am starting to worry if God is here, as if he is, they don't seem to be acting with God's love, do they? I can't bear it here anymore, Paul."

"Please don't cry, Laura. I am not going to marry Alice," I said, trying to calm her. "It is time for action and to hell with the consequences. I am ready to take my chances, are you? Would you like to meet up?"

"What, now?" asked Laura. "Where should we meet?"

"Let us link minds and focus on somewhere very nice. Have you thought of a place you would like to be?" I encouraged Laura.

"Yes, I have an image in my mind," confirmed Laura. "It is on a beach in the West Indies; It is in St. Lucia, with a turquoise sea and beautiful palm trees gently swaying in the setting sun. It is on a remote beach, so we are alone together. Can you visualise my image in your mind, Paul?"

"Yes, I can," I said. "Let's do it; let's go there right now. I can't bear another minute without seeing your beautiful face, Laura."

"You do know the Elders will find us and when they do, we will be expelled from the New Order. It will be the end for us. You do know that, don't you, Paul?"

"I do, Laura. I know what's coming, so every moment I have left with you has to count," I replied. "One moment with you is worth more than a thousand years of misery in eternity. You make my world go round. Are you ready?"

"Yes. This is the point of no return," said Laura. "Count to three and then let us execute our thoughts. We are on that beach in St. Lucia."

With that, in a blink of an eye, myself and Laura were on this beautiful, idyllic beach with a beautiful turquoise sea rolling in a nice gentle breeze and the palm trees swaying, cooling the hot sun shining down on us. It was a very fitting scene for what was very likely to be our last moments on this Earth, this New Order. We had to make every moment together count.

"This place is so beautiful," exclaimed Laura.

"So are you," I told her. "This is my greatest wish come true to be with you once again."

"It is mine as well," admitted Laura. "Shall we have a swim in the sea?"

"Yes. Last one in is a wuss," I replied, before admiring Laura in her bikini. She looked perfection personified in a human body.

"Are you coming in or are you going to just stand there gawping?" teased Laura.

"I'm sorry, I was so transfixed," I said, feeling very bashful before joining her in the sea. It was lovely to see Laura happy and relaxed and so was I. It was lovely to feel undiluted joy again and feel the adrenalin cruising through my veins again as I swam around Laura in the sea with the waves breaking into my face. For that glorious moment in time, we did not have a care in the world as Laura beckoned me over to her.

"It is time we had a kiss, Paul," she urged. "Let's make this moment really count."

One thing led to another and the inevitable happened. We were making passionate love in the sea. This was the moment I had been waiting for since I first law Laura that day at Theocratic School. It felt like what Heaven was truly about; I had truly found Heaven. This glorious moment I wished could be frozen in time forever but it was about to come to an abrupt halt as Laura noticed four well-suited gentlemen on the shore shaking their heads in complete disdain at us.

"Uh-oh, we have company," said Laura. "I guess fun time is over; it is time to face the music."

I looked round to see Ewan, Levi, Tony the Hawk and Jefferson shaking their heads in disgust as they summoned us back to shore. We were in massive trouble but we were past caring. I was no longer scared, nor was Laura. It was time to face our punishment as Jefferson declared, "Your time in the New Order is coming to an end. You have both committed a gross violation and will be expelled imminently. We are not cold-hearted; you can have family or friends present at the Tree of Eternal Judgment as you are released from this New Order. We will even allow you to go together; we just want to get rid of both of you now.

Laura and I went willingly to the Tree of Eternal Judgment. We were resigned to our fate as we held hands. My mum, dad, Dean and Amy Jane had already arrived at the Tree of Judgment and Dean was inconsolable.

"Dad, dad! Please don't go. I love you, dad. Tell them you are truly sorry; tell them that you are truly repentant. Please, dad, say it. I don't want you to go, Please!" he pleaded.

"Yes, please say you're sorry, Paul," pleaded Amy Jane. "We all love you so much. We do not want you to go. Please don't leave us."

"Son, I am so sorry you couldn't find the happiness you deserved in the Righteous Class," said dad. "I will miss you very much."

"I love you too, son," said mum, agonising between the love she had for me, her son, but unable to let go of her strong beliefs. "But it is for the best. I will miss you forever."

The Elders then bound Laura's hand to mine and clasped them together as they prepared our hands to make contact with the Tree of Eternal Judgment. No human flesh, perfect or imperfect, could withstand the electricity generated on contact with the Tree of Eternal Judgment. In truth it was a massive conductor and as our contact with it inched closer to our imminent demise, I leaned towards Laura to kiss her. I wanted our lips locked as we perished. I had one last thing to tell her before they did, "Laura, it has been the most wonderful honour anyone could have had to be your boyfriend. I love you."

"Ditto," was all the Time Laura had to reply as we hurriedly locked lips as contact was made with the Tree of Eternal Judgment and its surge of electricity pulsated in our bodies, pulverising us from the New Order.

We had gone, we were history! Paul was no more, Laura was no more, as Jefferson declared,

"You are the weakest links. Goodbye! Good riddance!"

Was this really the end, or was this a new beginning?

CHAPTER 8

BACK BEFORE MY TIME

1st October 2000, 1 am. Royal Derby Hospital

"Again!" urged the family and friends all gathered intently around my bedside as the defibrillator began to have an effect on me. "Again!" they cried in unison. "It's working! He's coming around, Paul's coming around! He is back with us; he's alive!"

The electric current supplied by the defibrillator had clearly done the trick. It had restarted my heart when all hope seemed lost. I started to hazily focus on the scene around me as I gradually sensed where I was. "Why am I in a hospital bed? Why are you all gathered around me? What is going on?"

"Paul, you were involved in a bad car accident," said mum, as she lovingly cradled my hand. Everyone around me was in tears. "You were catapulted through the car windscreen and laid dying on the floor. They said for two minutes you were actually dead. You were saved by a passer-by who, very fortunately, was an expert in CPR. She saved your life. If it wasn't for her, you would be dead. She is a nurse and she works here. She will be here in a minute to say hello to you. It will be a chance for you to say thank you to her for saving your life. It was touch and go, even until now, as you woke up."

"I thought we had lost you, dad," said Dean as he flung his arms tightly around me, bursting into tears.

"The nurse's actions provided critical time for you to still be alive when the air helicopter picked you up and rushed you to hospital," explained mum. "Her CPR saved your life but even then there were so many times when it looked like you had gone. It looked like your predicament was terminal, especially now, as you went into cardiac arrest. We are all so incredibly relieved you have come around," said a highly emotional mum.

"It is good to see you showing emotion again, mum," I told her.

"What do you mean, Paul?" mum asked me, all confused.

"In the New Order you were very unemotional. You were part of the Righteous Class as one of God's Onlookers," I said.

"New Order? New Order? What do you mean, the New Order?" they all asked as one as I realised I must have been having the most crazy dream in my comatose state. I had obviously been hallucinating; I must have been, I thought, as they all asked me about this New Order.

"Mum, you were married to an Elder called Ewan. You were young again, as was dad. He had got Pammie Anderson as his new girlfriend," I said. "It was all set in the future, our future on this Earth."

"I like the sound of being young again," replied mum. "It sounds a wonderful New Order to me. I am sure your dad would have loved Pammie Anderson as his girlfriend if he hadn't been married to me. I could see myself marrying again as I do miss your dad, I miss having a companion."

"What do you mean, mum?" I asked her, feeling very troubled. "Where is dad? Is he at home? He's not here; I know he was poorly when I left home this morning; I always feel so sorry for him, having had that stroke. In the New Order, dad was young and healthy again and told me he passed away in the year 2010, ten years after me, so he lived on for a good few years."

"Paul? Your dad is dead. Can't you remember? He passed away a year ago to the day you had your accident. What is it about the 30th September? I hate that day; it seems like it's cursed, don't you think? Please tell us more about this New Order; it sounds very interesting," urged mum.

I wasn't sure I wanted to, as why couldn't I remember dad passing away? How could I have forgotten such an important event? I thought my memory was playing a trick on me. Was I really awake?

"Please tell us more," urged Dean. "Was I there in this New Order?"

"Yes you were, Dean, and you were married to my Amy Jane. You were grown up by now," I told him. "You were a babe magnet."

"What!" exclaimed my horrified son. "I am only 14 years old! I don't think I want to hear this. I am not getting married, no way!"

"I don't think I am the sort of girl to ever betray someone's heart," protested Amy Jane. "I love you, Paul. How could I be with your son, Dean?"

"It's a long story but you were loyal, It's just that you didn't think I would be alive again, so you moved on," I told her.

"Was this New Order everything we would want it to be?" asked mum. "Tell us more; what was it like?"

"The whole world was a paradise and all the wicked and selfish people had gone from it. All the animals were no longer scared of us and roaming around everywhere. They were all tame and friendly, even the lions. You even had a pet lion in your garden. You had a palatial home; it was like a palace. We all had perfect bodies and we could teleport anywhere just by the power of thought alone and we could also communicate by thought alone. There was no ageing or dying or even pain in our bodies. I even got used to vegetarianism, as eating meat was now banned as we couldn't harm animals anymore. There was very much a plant-based diet going on."

"I do not like the sound of that," protested Dean. "You know how much I love my KFC or McDonalds. A world without them sucks."

"Oh, I don't know," interrupted Amy Jane. "I like the sound of no more animals being killed for food."

"How were Liverpool doing in the New Order, dad?" asked Dean. "Was Liverpool winning the Champions League again or the Premier League? What was Anfield now like? You know how much I love Liverpool."

"There was no Liverpool, no Villa, no Premier League, Dean," I answered. "I didn't see any football being played."

"What kind of New Order was that?" said a disgusted Dean. "If that is our future, you can count me out."

"There were big compensations, Dean," I explained. "Teleporting would have blown your mind; you could go anywhere in an instant. It was incredible; it was so much better than your virtual reality headsets or smartphones."

"What are you on about, dad?" asked Dean. "What are smartphones and the virtual reality gadgets you are mentioning? I haven't heard of them."

"I am sorry, son," I said. "I forgot I was in the year 2000. They haven't arrived yet, have they? It's all Nintendo and Sony Playstation, isn't it, with you?"

"Yes, dad," Answered Dean. "What are smartphones? Who told you about them? Is FIFA soccer even better on them? You know I love my FIFA soccer."

"Your gran, my mum, told me all about them," I answered. "Your gran mentioned a lot of things."

Everybody looked at mum with wonderment.

"Don't look at me," mum said. "I know nothing."

What did Nanna say about smartphones and the other things?" asked Dean. "What could they do?"

"Your nanna said they could do everything. You could contact anybody on social media sites like Facebook, Twitter or Instagram. You could post messages, videos or photos as well. You could also Google anything you wanted if you wanted to know something," I told him.

"What's a Google?" asked Dean. "What's Twitter? What's Instagram? It all sounds very exciting; I'm very excited."

"I love the sound of it, too," said Amy Jane. "I think Facebook is going to be my thing alright. I am definitely going to sign up when it comes and Instagram. I love my friends; I love talking. It sounds very cool. I can't wait for it."

"Nana said there will be an absolute explosion of technology in the last days," I explained. "There will be a lot that both of you will enjoy so much if she's right."

"I really don't know what you're talking about, Paul. I really haven't a clue what I was supposed to have told you," said mum. "I think your imagination is in overdrive. You have always had a weird and wonderful imagination, haven't you? I think you losing consciousness has made you a bit delirious; I am worried about you, Paul. Anyway, what is all this about the last days?"

"Yes, what is all this about the last days?" asked Dean. "It doesn't sound good, that I do know."

"Nanna said the world would end in 30 years' time. There would be a great war between good and evil and the good people won and inherited the Earth with God's help. Nanna warned the world would heat up, there would be two big viruses 10 years apart and that a lot of people would end up like they said in *2 Timothy 3*," I answered.

"Has anybody got a Bible?" asked Amy Jane.

"I have," answered mum. "I keep it in my bag. I don't know why, but now it seems useful. I will look up *2 Timothy 3*."

"What does it say?" asked Amy Jane.

"Oh my goodness, it describes how a lot of people become intolerant and rude and selfish, all sorts of things. I can kind of see it already today. Maybe I do know something after all," mum said.

"In the New Order, you said that not only were you a God's onlooker, Dean and Amy Jane became Onlookers as well and that was so vital as the world was hit by violent cosmic storms in the time of the end. Nanna said you all had to have faith in God to survive and you did. It was of the utmost importance," I disclosed.

"Wow! It sounds really scary," said Dean. "I am almost hoping Nanna isn't right in everything."

"I am glad I was brave if your mum is right, Paul," said Any Jane. "I am a right scaredy cat; I run a mile if I see a spider."

"I can't imagine being an onlooker as you call it. It doesn't seem my thing," said Dean. "I guess if Nanna's right, all sorts of freaky things will happen, won't it? I was looking forward to joining the army in a couple of years, so I wanted an exciting life. It sounds like it is going to be a lot more exciting life than I imagined."

"I think I can imagine myself as one of God's Onlookers," said mum. "I do identify with the whole ethos."

"They were very righteous in the New Order," I explained. "They were teachers; they taught people like me that had been reborn. They were, I would say, quite privileged. It was such an aspiration to be in the Righteous Class until it got a little weird."

"What do you mean, a little weird?" asked Dean.

"You had to go to Theocratic School and pass a Theocratic course. You had to prove your faith, which I did, but once I did, you got to go to a Righteous Convention and everybody there was naked. Mum was naked, you were naked, Amy Jane was naked, dad was naked. I was clothed, but had to get naked in front of everyone once I was baptised," I explained. "Apparently that is how everybody will live out their lives eventually in the New Order."

"What!" shouted an outraged Dean. "I am going to go to no New Order! Me, naked forever? No thanks!"

"I am not sure if it's for me, either," said Amy Jane. "I am very shy."

"Everybody had great bodies, everybody was in perfect shape," I explained. "There were no flabby bottoms to be seen anywhere. The women were like goddesses and the men were perfectly sculptured. We all had six packs. The Elders had six packs. All the women were a size 8 or 10. There was perfection all around. It was like a world full of adonises and aphrodites."

"Count me in!" declared Amy Jane, suddenly sounding very enthusiastic.

"It's still gross!" complained Dean. There was no persuading him yet. "I am not getting my kit off for any New Order!"

"I can't see it," said mum. "It's not for me either, I can't see me being naked."

"You were so happy at the Convention," I told her. "You were in your element. You were there to see me eventually married off. I was so angry with you."

"I thought Amy Jane was with Dean now, wasn't she? So, who were you marrying? Why were you angry with me?" asked mum.

"Yes, who were you marrying, Paul?" asked a very irritated Amy Jane.

"Mum had been party to making me have an arranged marriage to an Elder's daughter called Alice. I hadn't even talked to her before we were naked at this Righteous Convention and yet I was expected to marry her and she wanted it in just a few days. She told me that was longer than most couples in the Righteous Class. She said we could teach 20 hours a day every day and be so happy together in eternal nakedness," I said, as Dean started bursting out laughing. "It's not funny, Dean. I was mortified. I had to go on the run."

"Yes, it definitely is not funny!" complained Any Jane. "I am not happy!"

I was just about to explain it was all about heartache, my heartache, over a girl called Laura which would have made Amy Jane even more upset, when there was a knock on the door of my private room.

"Can I come in?" said the nurse.

"Yes, of course. Come in, come in," my family said. "It is the special nurse that saved your life. She gave you vital CPR; she gave you the kiss of life."

"Hello, Paul, how are you today? How are you feeling?" she said.

I looked up and could hardly catch my breath. "It is you, Laura. I can't believe it! Oh my God, you were the girl who saved my life."

My family reacted in unison. "You already know Laura? It is a small world, isn't it?"

Amy Jane was not amused. "How do you know Laura? You never mentioned a Laura to me," she said, feeling very miffed.

"I don't know you, Paul," said Laura. "I have never known you. I was just happening to pass by when I saw this stricken man lying on the ground. There had been this terrible car accident and people were crying. You appeared dead; there was no sign of life in you, but as a nurse, I knew how to give effective CPR and I could feel the flickers of breath returning into you. Other than that, I have never met you in my life before. I wonder if the drugs you have been on has made you delirious? Let me check your pulse, Paul."

"I feel fine," I said. "My pulse is racing, I can feel it," I replied.

"So, Paul, what makes you think you know me?" asked Laura.

"Yes, Paul, please tell us! Please do tell us!" said Amy Jane angrily.

"Laura was with me in the New Order. When I couldn't have Amy Jane as she was married to Dean, I had to search for love again and I met Laura. She was with me at the end as I left the New Order. We had just ….., just ….."

"Go on, Paul, spit it out!" urged Amy Jane. "You had just what?"

I knew what I was about to say would devastate Amy Jane but I had dug a massive hole for myself. I had to finish my sentence; I had to tell the truth. It was the truth, wasn't it?

"We ....., we had just made love in the Caribbean Sea."

"You bastard!" said Amy Jane as she ran out of the room crying her eyes out.

"Paul, how could you?" said mum. "Whatever possessed you to say that? It is spiteful fantasy and not nice. How could you say that in front of Amy Jane? Didn't you realise how upset she would be? She has been beside herself with worry with you being at death's door and you torment her with this fantasy. It is not funny and it is not fair on her," she admonished me and she was right; what was I thinking?

"I am sorry, mum. I will explain everything to Amy Jane. I do love her and still do. I know it sounds like fantasy but it all seemed very real to me. It all felt very real." Everything I could recall seemed very credible, however much it appeared to be fantasy. It all felt crystal clear in my head and in such detail and yet my dad had told me he died in the year 2010 and that was not what I had just been told. I had remembered him being alive when I had my accident so what was fact and what was fiction? Laura was keen to probe me even more.

"That wasn't very nice of you to upset your girlfriend like that, Paul, was it? What makes you think you know me like you claim?" She asked.

"You told me you had a favourite romantic spot up a tree above the River Thames. You liked to have a kiss and a cuddle and a fumble up there with your boyfriend. You told me you were a very passionate feminist and had trouble recognising male authority which was very problematic in this New Order," I told her.

"Well, I am impressed," said Laura. "I am a feminist, a staunch feminist and I do love this romantic spot up this tree that stretches out of the River Thames. You have got most things right, Paul, but ....., but ....."

"But what?" I asked her.

"I don't have a boyfriend. I have never had a boyfriend. I love girls. I went up this tree with my girlfriend to have a kiss and a cuddle and a fumble. I have never wanted a boyfriend so I don't believe you as I don't want to ever have a boyfriend. The thought of sex with a man is gross. I am actually really upset you could think or even imagine I would make love with you. I'm going now."

"Please don't go," I pleaded. "I really didn't mean to insult you. I don't know what is happening to me; I am beginning to question my sanity as it did feel like love with you. I have met you before but I can't justify the logic and authenticity of what I am claiming but I would like to tell you that I am so grateful you saved my life. I thank you from the bottom of my heart. I owe you my life and this might seem like another bit of madness on my part but I want to do something for you in return as an act of gratitude."

"What's that?" asked Laura.

"You warned me about something in the New Order, something that will happen to you on the 16th November 2000. It might or might not happen, but I have to warn you. If I am right, it will save your life; if I am wrong, I can still look myself in the mirror and know I tried to do the right thing," I answered.

Laura felt chills filling her soul as she asked me, "What is supposed to happen? What have I supposed to have told you?"

"You told me you drowned on the 16th November. You died and that is why I could see you in the New Order. We were both reborn. You told me you fell from your favourite tree that stretched out over the River Thames. There had been so much rainy weather you said it must have had an influence in why your branch, a thick branch, suddenly snapped, releasing you into the river below," I told her.

"Wow!" was all Laura could say before trying to rubbish my claims. "I can swim like a fish; I wouldn't have drowned. I don't believe you."

"You knocked your head on another thick branch on the way down," I said. "It knocked you unconscious as you entered the river. You didn't swim, you sank to the bottom. You told me your boyfriend couldn't swim to help you."

"My girlfriend couldn't swim," Laura admitted. "I have got goosepimples all over. I don't want to believe you; you are actually upsetting me now. I must go."

"I am sorry, Laura, I didn't mean to upset you. I know it's very serious what I am claiming. I can understand why you want to leave. Please just bear it in mind. I don't want anything bad to happen to you. Even if it is all in my imagination, I can't be sure if it is," I pleaded with Laura as she left. I had done all I can and I sincerely hoped she had taken the warning seriously and that she wouldn't have that terrible accident. I owed her and although I could tell I really had strong feelings for her, even love, now I was back in the real world I knew my true love was Amy Jane. It even felt a relief that Laura was really into girls so my love for Amy Jane wasn't compromised anymore by feeling I was meant for Laura; I clearly wasn't. That was good but what wasn't good was that again something didn't seem right. In the New Order, Laura clearly loved men; she loved me and I would have sworn she had told me that before she drowned she was in that tree with a boyfriend. It was a complete mystery why certain things were now different. Why? Was I really going mad? First dad, now Laura. I was starting to feel very troubled as Amy Jane returned.

"You owe me an explanation, Paul," she demanded. "It had better be good!"

"I will tell you everything, Amy Jane," I said. "I had been awoken or reborn into a strange new environment where lots of familiar faces were in unfamiliar circumstances. I discovered that Dean had grown up into an impressive young man and somehow you were now his wife. I was utterly crestfallen, utterly devastated, as I loved you so much and I really didn't want to live in this world knowing I could no longer have you as you were in the arms of my son. I had to adapt to the new world somehow and I saw Laura. I was entranced by her personality and looks; I was so drawn to her and yes, we wanted to marry and we did make love, but if you weren't a married woman none of this would have happened. You are my true love, Amy Jane; no-one else, even Laura. I wouldn't have survived without her in this world, her companionship; her kiss was wonderful, I am not going to lie. It seemed to fill me with a lust to live life and then she was with me as I got electrified on the Tree of Eternal Judgment. The next thing I know I am coming round in this hospital."

"What was Laura's kiss like?" asked Amy Jane. "Why did it have such a big effect on you?"

"It was so passionate, so forceful. It was like I was being stimulated so much with her passion," I answered.

"Almost like the kiss of life. I wonder, I just wonder," said Amy Jane. "I think I'm beginning to understand."

"What are you beginning to understand?" I asked her.

"I think it was your subconscious mind at work and while Laura was giving you the kiss of life, it was interpretating it as a girl in love with you as you were in this dreamlike state. I see it now," declared Amy Jane. "And you waking up here with the defibrillator just after experiencing some sort of electrocution in that New Order of yours. It fits; you were just having an extravagant dream. I'm so relieved."

"I guess so," I replied. I wasn't going to argue with her; what was the point? I was back in the real world. I was back in reality. What was the point of tormenting myself with the New Order? What Amy Jane said made sense; it had to be an overreaction of my imagination, hadn't it? "I want to tell you something, Amy Jane."

"What do you want to tell me?" she replied.

"I was going to ask you to marry me yesterday," I told her. "I had bought you a ring. I had a special bouquet of flowers arranged to give to you and now look where I am. I am so sorry it has all ended up like this."

"You don't have to be sorry, Paul. I love you with all my heart," cried Amy Jane. "I would have been the happiest girl in the world to be your wife; I would have said yes to you in a heartbeat. I would love to wear your ring."

"Then, Amy Jane ......, will you marry me? Will you be my wedded wife?" I said, getting out of bed and onto one knee.

"Oh Paul, yes! Yes! Of course I will marry you," she yelled at the top of her voice, jumping up and down with a frenzied joy and delight.

Mum and Dean could hear the commotion and came back into my room.

"Are you alright, Amy Jane?" asked mum.

"We're getting married; Paul's asked me to marry him and I said yes!" said a very excited and emotional Amy Jane.

"Well congratulations to the both of you. I will start saving for a hat," said mum warmly.

"Yes, well done, dad," said Dean. "Amy Jane is well fit!"

It was the perfect end to what had been the most traumatic period of my life. I had been saved from death's door to having a marriage proposal to Amy Jane accepted. Life seemed good once more; what was there to worry about? I had gone before my time and come back before my time; was normality now restored?

7 months later (April 30th 2001)

Amy Jane and I were happier than we had ever been as we walked lovingly together hand in hand. We were a couple madly in love and all the weirdness of the New Order had well and truly gone back into the recesses of my mind as I fully immersed myself in the glorious present. I had the perfect girl alongside me; there was nothing troubling in our world, when Amy Jane spotted Laura walking gingerly in town.

"That's Laura. Let's go and say hello to her. I wonder how she is?" said Amy Jane.

"Yes, it is really good to see her around," I agreed.

"She is pregnant; she is carrying a bump. Oh my God, how exciting," noticed Amy Jane.

"Hello, Laura, it's fantastic to see you again," I said. "I am delighted to know you are alive and well; I will never forget I owe my life to you."

"I think I owe my life to you as well," declared Laura. "I took notice of what you told me about that tree and I am so glad I did, as that branch you predicted would break off did just that. It had completely snapped off. I could have been sitting on that branch. I went cold with shock, thinking did I really drown and had I seen you in the New Order? I went numb thinking I could have described my own death to you. I had noticed you had warned me about all the wet weather and it was really bad, wasn't it, last November? I decided to trust my gut instinct that you were telling me the truth, however fanciful, and I am so relieved I did. You are a lifesaver, Paul. Now look at me; I am pregnant. This baby would never be due to be born if I had that accident. I get so emotional when I think about it."

"How far gone are you?" asked Amy Jane.

"I am 7 months pregnant," answered Laura.

"Who is the daddy?" asked Amy Jane, unaware that Laura was not into boys.

"Yes, who is the daddy?" I asked Laura. I was curious to know, as I knew something Amy Jane didn't.

"It's ….., it's ….. er, artificial insemination," answered Laura as she struggled to answer. In truth, she didn't know how she got pregnant as she still hadn't had any relationships with any guy in this world. The answer sounded plausible to me as that would negate the need to be with a boy. I believed her; I wanted to believe her but I was doing the maths. 7 months pregnant meant she was impregnated around the end of September. What a coincidence; what an unfortunate coincidence. I told myself, Paul, stop being stupid.

"How has your other half taken it?" asked Amy Jane, suddenly realising Laura had given a weird answer. It was time for Amy Jane to be updated.

"I like girls, Amy Jane," revealed Laura. "My other half is insanely happy." That was a lie as Laura's other half had walked out in her. She had known nothing about Laura's artificial insemination; she had not been party to it and felt Laura had cheated on her.

"Are you having a boy or a girl?" asked Amy Jane, feeling happy that as Laura fancied girls, she was no longer a threat for my affections.

"I am having a girl," answered Laura. "I am going to call her Evie."

"That's a lovely name," said Amy Jane. "I am starting to feel broody," as she looked over at me. "I can't wait to be a mum myself. We're working on it very hard, aren't we, Paul?"

"Er ….. yes," I said, blushing bright red.

The girls laughed out aloud in joyous union. "I've got to go now. It has been so nice to see you again," said Laura.

"It has been so nice to see you as well," responded Amy Jane. "Please keep in touch. I would love to see your baby girl when she is born."

"Yes," hesitated Laura. "Of course. Maybe you could become godparents to her; we will have to see."

"That would be great if we were to become godparents to your little girl," I said. "It feels right, doesn't it?"

It all seemed very cordial between us but Laura had her child and moved away. We didn't know where she was and there was more than a twinge of regret that she had decided to go away. It seemed Laura was destined to be a very magical and mystical figure to me. I still couldn't help thinking about her little girl; she couldn't possibly be mine, could she? It was a ridiculous thought, but I couldn't get it out of my mind and I was seriously hoping Amy Jane hadn't been putting 2 and 2 together and making 5. She would be gutted if my misgivings were true and our beautiful harmony would be ruined maybe forever. Maybe Laura moving away was for the best as innocence can sometimes be bliss and make for a simple life. After all I had been through, a simple life seemed beautiful; it wasn't too much to ask for, was it?

END OF PART ONE

THE LIGHT IS DONE

NOW READ THE SHADE!

– Readers' Challenge –

(And at the end please declare
which part you preferred)

Please let me know

PART TWO

THE SHADE

THE MIRACLE
OF
LITTLE EVIE

(Beware, the bad man is coming!! But for who?)

CHAPTER 9

LIFE MOVES ON

July 2005

It had been four years since we last saw Laura and nearly five years since my tumultuous car accident, and it had all seemed a lifetime ago as I continued to live my life in innocent bliss. I was now a married man to my beloved Amy Jane. We married two years ago and were more in love than ever. There was only one thing niggling away on the horizon like a distant black cloud, and that was Amy Jane wanted a baby but she was having trouble conceiving. We lived in hope she could conceive in time but I had noticed it was beginning to trouble her.

My mum had become a fully-fledged member of God's Onlookers. She had become a very passionate follower; she kept telling us the world was in trouble and that God's Kingdom was coming to take over but we all seemed too immersed in our lives to take much notice of her. It was lovely to see mum so alive again and so full of verve; she seemed a different person to that person who had been nursing dad during his final days. When he had his stroke, mum had become very tired and worn down, I remembered, but I still couldn't remember my dad dying. I put it all down to head injuries suffered in that car accident where, for a short period, it had seemed I was dead and not part of a deeper mystery. It continued to trouble me all the same that my dad died and I couldn't recall going to his funeral but I tried to block it out by putting everything into my relationship and marriage to Amy Jane, and for the most part it had worked. We were a beautiful couple in love; Amy Jane was literally my world. I was so grateful I had a second chance of life or I could never have known such happiness. Could it last?

Dean, my beloved son, had joined the army. He worked hard and he played hard. Dean was only 18 years old but the army had made him into a man. Dean had turned into a babe magnet and was so happy playing the field. He was loving them and leaving them but had also grown so strong physically and mentally and that made me so proud. But now he had just been posted to Afghanistan and that really made me nervous as I had seen it on TV and it seemed like a hellhole. What also began to trouble me was when I was in my coma in my hospital bed, I could still remember mum telling me how the world would evolve while talking to her in that paradise New Order. I could clearly remember her telling me about the rise of Al-Qaeda and the Twin Towers. That had happened as she foretold me, and another thing she had prophesised to me that seemed to be coming true was the rise of Facebook and the online world. I couldn't get Amy Jane off this new phenomenon; she was a highly sociable and vivacious lady. She loved it. I sometimes thought I was living in a movie world where I suspected what was coming next and yet other times I would get hit by a curveball, like Laura's sexual origins. I still, to this day, couldn't believe she only liked girls, as when I was with her in the New Order our love felt very real. Indeed, making love with her in the Caribbean Sea felt so natural and her passion and want for me was so evident in her.

I couldn't help thinking about Laura. We hadn't seen her for 4 years; how was she? How was her baby girl? She would be 4 years old now. I wondered what she was like. I hoped Laura and her baby girl were happy; it seemed strange they weren't part of our world but this was about to change in a big way! Contact was about to be made to me from a very special person and by a very unexpected source; it would rock my world to its core and make me realise more than ever I was living in a much stranger world than I thought, a world where I could not presume anything anymore.

I had not been sleeping well lately. I kept having vivid dreams of seeing myself being a dad again with a daughter. I kept dreaming of her playing on the swing and slides and her happily skipping along with such beautiful joy and enthusiasm. It felt so warm inside when this little girl called me daddy. I loved my dreams but it was making me feel so tired, like it was really affecting my sleep cycle. I felt so drained it was like I hadn't achieved any sleep at all. It seemed my imagination had completely swamped my ability to sleep, but was it just imagination? I was about to get the shock of my life as Amy Jane and I were in Venice having such a glorious break together, having enjoyed a beautiful gondola ride over the canals of Venice. It was that night my innocent world changed forever!

CHAPTER 10

EVIE

It was 3 a.m. in the morning. I had been tossing and turning all night when I shot up in stunned silence and shock. I could hear something; a strange voice in my head that most definitely wasn't mine was making itself heard. It was that of a little girl. It was saying "Daddy ....., daddy."

I rubbed my eyes and looked at the clock, It was 3 a.m. There was no-one around apart from myself and Amy Jane, who was blissfully asleep, completely oblivious to anything I was hearing. I urged myself to get a grip and for goodness sake go back to sleep and to hell with my imagination. It was getting out of control now; I really had to do something about it. I had settled back down when it happened again.

"Daddy ....., daddy ....., why won't you answer me, daddy?"

I again shot up from my pillow. I was getting flustered now. "Who is this? What do you want?"

"Daddy ....., daddy ....., I miss you, daddy," said the voice.

"Who are you?" I said angrily. "I am not your daddy."

"You are daddy! You are my daddy!" said the voice.

"What's your name, little girl?" I asked the voice.

"I am Evie, my name is Evie. You are not angry with me, are you, daddy?" the voice said as she started crying.

"Don't cry," I said. "I am not angry with you. Just go to sleep. I am sure I will meet you soon."

By now Amy Jane had woken up hearing my commotion. "Paul, what is it? Calm down. Are you having a nightmare? Who were you talking to? You were talking to someone and it sounded like you were talking to a little girl. I am starting to worry about you, Paul. Your dreaming is getting terrible now."

"I am really sorry, Amy Jane; I did not mean to wake you. I was having a bad dream. I am sorry; I dreamt I was a dad again and it led me to talking in my sleep," I explained.

"You looked awake to me," said Amy Jane.

"I was still in a dreamlike state; I just had my eyes opened, that's all," I told her, desperately hoping to spin myself out of trouble and hope that she believed me. For the rest of the night, I just laid awake in turmoil with my thoughts. I couldn't get back to sleep again; how could you after that? I really hoped the voice wouldn't return as I would have to ignore it as Amy Jane would go mad if she heard me talking again. Was it really Evie calling me daddy? Was it Laura's daughter that was calling me daddy? How could I be her daddy when I never had sex with her mummy, at least not in this world, this reality, but I had in the New Order. Surely that couldn't be the explanation could it if somehow Evie was right. How could I hear Evie's voice when I was in Venice with Amy Jane? How could it possibly really be Evie when I didn't know where she and her mum were? I had never seen Evie in my life; I didn't know what she looked like even. How could she claim I was her daddy? There were so many unanswered questions but the one thing I did know was if Evie was right in calling me her daddy I was in trouble with Amy Jane. How could she believe anything I said if I was proved to be a daddy to another person's child? The stakes were enormous.

I needed breathing space as I told Amy Jane I needed to sleep in the spare room. I couldn't take the chance I would implicate myself if Evie's voice in my head returned. Amy Jane didn't complain as I was beginning to affect her sleep but urged me to get help. I was really worried how to handle all this as could I dare to believe I was a dad to a little girl? I had always wanted a daughter but not at the expense of the love of my life, Amy Jane. It was not long before the ante was only going to get more serious as I prepared to receive a phone call out of the blue.

"Hello, who is this?" I asked.

"It's me, Laura. Paul, we need to talk."

"Is that really you, Laura? I haven't seen you for ages," I replied. "Why do we need to talk?"

"It's my little girl, Evie. She is convinced you are her daddy. I know it sounds fanciful and I have tried to talk to her that it can't be, but I don't know who the daddy is or how I got pregnant in the first place. I really don't know what to think. Can you come and visit?"

"Where are you? Where are you living?" I asked her.

"In Bristol, I live in Bristol. I had to get away from Derby as I was so upset at being pregnant and not knowing how I could be, and all that stuff you told me about the new order just freaked me out, I couldn't cope. I wanted to have my daughter alone; I had lost my girlfriend, I was mortified, I needed space. Me and Evie have been safe and having a great time as mother and daughter. It is only recently Evie has been acting strangely and it has made me think I have to get to the bottom of what she is claiming as I can't be sure she is not right. Evie is a very special girl; she seems to know things. She is a very clever girl and highly individual. I think you will be entranced by her; she seems to have special qualities."

"What do you mean?" I asked Laura.

"Evie can communicate by thought; I can hear her thoughts." She replied.

"I have something to tell you, Laura," I said, realising now it really was Evie, her little girl that had contacted me in Venice. I could hear Evie's thoughts. She couldn't have possibly known I was in Venice. It appeared not to matter to her where I was, it was who I was. Distance was no issue when you could transmit thought to any location. Apparently, all she had to do was visualise who she wanted to contact and it was me. "I have to tell you Evie has already contacted me. I was in Venice and she was adamant I was her daddy," I said.

"I can believe it," said Laura. "Evie is such a special girl. She is not normal; she has an enormous sixth sense that makes her so aware. If she says you are her daddy we have to take her seriously. I did tell her not to scare you with her thoughts invading your mind but it looks like she ignored me. She is a naughty girl but I love her. She wanted to speak to the person she believes is her daddy."

"She does sound a special girl," I admitted. "I do have to admit I am excited to see her. I will see you soon and we can have a catch up. It is best I come alone as until we get to the bottom of it I think Amy Jane would find it very hard to accept."

"I fully agree, It is for the best," said Laura.

"Can I ask you one last question before I go?" I asked her. "Please tell me how and when she told you she thought I was her daddy. What made her think that?"

"It was only recently Evie started asking questions about why I was not with her daddy," explained Laura. "It is very hard telling your young daughter you are not into men, but I tried my best. Evie could read my thoughts as I started explaining it to her and she could tell that I didn't know who her daddy was and the only ludicrous explanation to me of what was basically an immaculate conception was what you told me that we made love in the New Order. She could tell I was visualising your image as I explained this to her. She knew what you looked like and could focus her young mind on your image when beginning to targeting her thoughts. It was like she could download images from my mind. The rest is history; you heard her. There is one other weird thing I want to tell you."

"What's that?"

"When I mentioned the words 'New Order', she just stopped me there. Evie said that was where she was from. Evie said she came from the New Order. I had to contact you, didn't I, when I heard that? It is freaking me out, Paul," revealed Laura. "I am scared; I don't know what to think. Will you take a DNA test?"

"Don't worry, Laura. I am coming to see you," I comforted her. "I need to know for my own sanity as well."

I awaited my DNA results with baited breath as I continued to live my life in complete uncertainty. It was making me so quiet with worry and Amy Jane had really started to pick up on it. I hated keeping things from her but for now it was kinder to go on the ethos of what you don't know can't hurt you. I didn't want Amy Jane to suffer and I knew I was in a no-win situation if

Evie was proven to be my daughter as I knew I would lose Amy Jane. I wanted to cross that bridge when it came to it as if I really did have a daughter, I would have to be responsible and accountable for my actions. And if Evie wasn't my daughter, part of me was already going to be so gutted. Evie sounded the most sweet and delightful little girl and one with very special gifts so not to be her daddy after all this drama was going to feel so anti-climactic, especially as Amy Jane was not any closer to getting hers and mine's baby. Everything was so bittersweet and then the results came in; I was Evie's daddy; she was right! I didn't know whether to laugh or cry!

It was time to face the music. First, I needed to go and see my daughter for the first time. Just how special was she? I was also looking forward to seeing Laura for the first time in over 4 years. Had she changed much? I wasn't to realise that this was going to be the last time I saw Laura alive ever again!!

As I approached Laura's house in Bristol I was filled with enormous guilt as I felt so elated in seeing my new daughter for the first time. To see that girl who had so lovingly and sweetly called me her daddy was going to be a joy to behold and yet I felt so apprehensive at the same time as how could all this be possible? I had only met Laura and made love to her in my comatose state and not in this real world. Could the New Order really be real? Could it really be I was more than dreaming when I was in the New Order? There was one thing that was for sure, I had a daughter and I was now at Laura's house. There was no going back now as I rung the bell.

"Come in, Paul," said Laura. "It's been a long time, hasn't it?"

"It is so good to see you again," I replied.

"You too, Paul. I am glad you're here. Do you want to meet Evie?"

"Absolutely," I said.

"Daddy! Daddy!" shrieked Evie. "You've come to see me, daddy!" Evie was skipping and dancing up and down with joy. She was so excited to see me and it made me feel so warm and special inside. I instantly knew we had a special bond, a very special bond between us.

"Daddy, have you come to play? Do you want to see my dolls?" Evie urged me.

"I am sure daddy would love to see your dolls, sweetheart," said Laura, "but me and daddy need to talk first and then daddy will come and play."

"Yes, Evie, I will," I said. "Let me talk to your mummy first."

"Okay," said Evie as she bounced out of the room with such delightful glee. "Don't take too long."

"Paul, you need to tell me what you know," urged Laura. "What was this New Order that Evie says she is from and that you were going on about so much in hospital that day? It is becoming clear that it is very spooky how real it seems. You told me I was going to die and I would have done if you hadn't warned me. How could you know that if it hadn't already happened and I had actually told you? You said we made love in the sea; I actually do believe you now, Paul. Evie is living proof. Somehow, the New Order transcends the reality we now live in. Please tell me more about us in the New Order as I can't understand how it has got to this."

"Of course I will tell you everything I know," I replied. "I first met you at Theocratic School and I was instantly drawn to you. I loved your slim figure and brunette hair. I romanced you; I respected you. Our first date was to see the gorillas in the mist."

"What? Please stop there, Paul," said Laura. "This sounds wonderful. I like it that you respected me and romanced me as most men don't respect girls. I think that is one of the reasons I like girls better; men patronised me, they only wanted me for one thing so the fact you took time to get to know me, I am impressed. I could see myself liking you, although not enough to make love to you yet. You said our first date was to see the gorillas in the mist; was that at some kind of zoo?"

"No, Laura, it was in the jungles of Rwanda in Africa," I replied. "It was in their real habitat."

"What?" said Laura. "That sounds a brilliant first date. Did we fly out there and then get a guide?"

"No. We teleported to see the gorillas. We got there in the blink of an eye," I answered her.

"What? That sounds incredible," said Laura. "I can't believe it; tell me more."

"We could teleport by the power of thought alone," I told her. "We had perfect bodies; we could do anything. We could communicate with other by thought alone; we could read thoughts."

"That's amazing, that's truly amazing," Laura eulogised.

"You held a baby gorilla in your arms and the mummy gorilla let you and I was with you until I went swinging in the trees on the back of the daddy gorilla," I told her.

"Aah, it sounds so wonderful I could cry," said an emotional Laura. "I had a cute baby gorilla in my arms; I was cradling a cute baby gorilla! I can't believe it; it sounds unbelievable. How come the mummy gorilla let me hold her baby? I would have thought she would not let me. She would have wanted to rip my arms off, wouldn't she?"

"All the animals were tame in the New Order," I explained to Laura. "There was now a complete trust between humans and animals. We didn't harm animals and they didn't harm us. All the humans became Vegan; nobody ate meat anymore. The animals, all of them, grew to love us and trust us."

"I love this New Order," exclaimed Laura. "I want to live there. I am Vegan, so is Evie; we love animals. I can imagine being so happy there."

"It was literally a paradise, a massive worldwide Garden of Eden," I told her.

"So, this is the world Evie says she is from and I believe her. She really is, isn't she? Oh my God!" screamed Laura, "Evie can read thoughts and she can speak to people with her thoughts; oh my God! I have a super special daughter; we have a super special daughter. I did let you make love to me, didn't I?"

"Yes. We fell in love with each other eventually," I answered. "We weren't supposed to make love to each other; it was forbidden as I had become Righteous and you had remained Unrighteous. I was promised to another girl, a Righteous girl but we loved each other so much by then we couldn't bear to live part. We disobeyed the rules and got sent to the Tree of Eternal Judgment where our spirits were electrocuted. That was when I came round in hospital."

"Oh my God!" said Laura, open-mouthed, before asking, "why did you become Righteous and I stayed Unrighteous?"

"You were a rebel, Laura," I told her. "All the males were in charge; females had to be in subjection. You couldn't or wouldn't accept it so you never got into the Righteous Class."

"Wow! That so sounds like me," said Laura. "I really believe all this happened; oh my God! Thank you so much for explaining it all."

"Daddy! I can't wait much longer!" shouted an impatient Evie. "Have you finished talking to mummy yet?"

"He will be with you in a minute, sweetheart, We're nearly finished," shouted Laura. "Where do we go from here, Paul? I feel like a modern-day Mary; I have had an immaculate baby just like she did. I like girls but I could see myself falling for you; you are my baby girl's father after all, aren't you?"

I didn't know how to answer that as however much I loved and cared for Laura, my love for Amy Jane was stronger. I was a married man; I was married to Amy Jane. I loved her so much and yet I was a dad to a wonderful little girl called Evie. She was such a lovely innocent bundle of unbridled joy and delight but how innocent was she? Evie was a product of the New Order and yet she was living on this earth. It was time to get to know her.

"I love your dolls, Evie. They are very pretty, aren't they?" I asked her.

"Yes, daddy. I like making them pretty," said Evie.

"You are a very clever girl, aren't you, Evie?" I replied. "You can talk to daddy when he's not there, can't you?"

"It is easy, daddy," said Evie. "All I have to do is close my eyes, daddy."

"That is wonderful, Evie," I replied. "Can you do anything else?"

"I can move places," answered Evie.

"Where have you been, Evie?" I asked her.

"I can go from my bedroom to mummy's bedroom without walking. I can just appear," said Evie.

"Wow! That's clever, Evie, that's really clever," I told her. "Can you go further than that?"

"I haven't tried yet, daddy," Evie told me. "Mummy says I shouldn't."

"Mummy is quite right," I told her.

"Daddy, can I come to see you?" asked Evie.

"Of course," I said, knowing and worrying how Amy Jane would react, but how could I turn down my own daughter?

"Where do you live, daddy?" asked Evie.

"I live in a place near Derby," I told her. "It's called El Campo."

"Daddy, that's a funny name for a house," laughed Evie. "Have you got a picture of it?"

"Yes, Evie. I will show it you on my phone. There it is," I said.

"It's a nice house, daddy," replied Evie. "I would like to live there."

"But Evie, your mummy would not like that. What about mummy?" I asked her, feeling very troubled at how she wasn't thinking about her mummy.

"There's a bad man coming," was Evie's chilling reply.

"What do you mean there's a bad man coming, Evie?" I asked her, feeling very disturbed. "What bad man? Where? When?"

Evie couldn't answer. All she could say was there was a bad man coming. It seemed like she was having a cryptic premonition, a heightened sixth sense of something bad waiting to happen but where and to whom?

As I left Bristol that night I was a mixture of awe and wonder and fear and dread. My life was not going to be the same again. Evie had and was going to transform my life.

I had faced the music with Laura and Evie and I now had to face my biggest test; what on earth did I say to Amy Jane? How on earth did I put it to her I was a dad to Laura's little girl, Evie, when Amy Jane hadn't been able to conceive herself? Amy Jane was going to be absolutely devastated. How could I ever be forgiven by her? To think my protestations and explanations in the hospital that she had nothing to be worried about had now resulted in her partner actually being a father to a new daughter, it was going to be too much for her to bear. I hadn't cheated on her in this reality but how the hell was she going to believe that? I felt like a man on death row as I approached Amy Jane that evening.

"I have something to tell you, Amy Jane; something I never wanted to ever tell you in my life. You have to believe me when I say I love you more than any girl I have met in my life. I would die for you; I have always said that but …., but ……"

"But what, Paul? You're worrying me. What's wrong? What do you need to tell me?" asked a highly stressed Amy Jane.

"There is no easy way to say this, but ….., but …..," I stuttered.

"What is it? Spit it out, Paul," urged an agitated Amy Jane.

"I have found out I am a dad. I am so sorry, Amy Jane. I am so really sorry. I did not know until today," I said, with trepidation, as I awaited Amy Jane's reaction.

"You bastard," she cried hysterically. "You utter bastard! How could you? How could you do this to me? I thought you loved me; you knew how much I wanted to have your baby and now you tell me you've impregnated somebody else. Who is she? Who is she? Who is she? Tell me!! Tell me!!," shouted Amy Jane, who by now was hyperventilating with volcanic fury. "I hope she is worth it, Paul. Tell me who she is; if you ever loved me you would at least tell me that much."

"It is Laura. I have just found out Evie is my daughter," I told her. "I didn't believe it as I have never been unfaithful to you in this world. I would never knowingly cheat on you if you were mine but somehow what happened in the New Order has translated itself into real life. I am so sorry; I don't know what else to say."

Amy Jane just stood there speechless with incandescent anger etched on her face as she took in what I had told her and then carefully prepared her response and it was going to cut me more precisely than the most experienced surgeon as she delivered a fatal blow to our marriage.

"Paul, our marriage is over. I can't accept what you have done. You insult me by expecting me to believe it is all to do with the New Order. How could you think I could be that stupid to believe that rubbish? You are welcome to Laura; you can have her and her daughter. I am out of here; it is goodbye! Don't come after me, Paul, or I will make you wish you were back in that New Order. Do you understand?"

"I do but I will always love you whatever you might think of me," I replied. "I am telling you the truth but how could I expect you to ever believe me? I know it sounds preposterous, but I do have a daughter now and I have responsibilities. I can't escape that; you wouldn't expect me to. I love you and never, ever, wanted to hurt you. I love you so much. I know you have to go; I won't stop you. You deserve so much better," I said, fighting back my tears.

"Do you know, there was this guy at work called Bradley. He is only young, but he is crazy for me. He was always asking me if he could take me out, even though I was a married lady. He was like a good-looking young Brad

Pitt but I never wavered; I was loyal to you. You were my husband; I loved you and thought you loved me. Well, I am going to say yes to Bradley now; I am going to be a free girl now," revealed Amy Jane.

I cried like a baby. I had lost Amy Jane and who could blame her? I had lost the love of my life to the consequences of something I did in what seemed another world. It was not going to be long before another even worse event was going to happen!

16th November 2005 – Bristol (Laura's place)

"Mummy, can we go out today?" pleaded Evie. "I don't want to be here today. Can we go out?"

"We can't, honey," replied Laura. "I am expecting somebody. We can't go out today. Maybe tomorrow."

"But mummy, we need to go out," urged Evie. "A bad man is coming; I don't want him to come. He is a bad man, mummy."

"But it is only the boiler man, sweetheart. If we don't get our boiler fixed we are going to get very cold, It is winter soon," said Laura. "If he comes soon and gets the boiler fixed, I promise you we will go out."

"But mummy, he is coming to get you," cried Evie.

"Honey, you are being silly. I have to get our boiler fixed or we won't be warm. Please stop being silly," admonished Laura.

"If the man knocks on your door three times, please don't answer the door, mummy. Please, please, mummy," pleaded Evie.

Laura was just about to agree when the boiler man arrived. The knock on the door was repeated and then repeated again. It had knocked three repetitive times like Evie had warned.

"Don't open the door, mummy. The bad man is here," warned Evie. "He's come for you; don't open the door, mummy."

Laura should have listened to her daughter, she really should have listened, but she didn't. In the heat of the moment she opened the door to him, the boiler man, but was he really a boiler man? Laura had let her worry over her boiler supersede her daughter's warning. Evie was distressed and ran upstairs. she was only a little girl; she wasn't ready to be able to protect mummy as the boiler man introduced himself to Laura.

"Hello, I am Winston. I am here to fix your boiler. Would you like to show me where it is?"

Laura invited him in to show him where it was but was unaware that Winston had something wrapped up inside his left hand, inside a handkerchief. It was some sort of paralysing agent. Winston was not a boiler man at all, like Evie feared; he was a kind of hitman, but who had sent him? The paralysing agent was applied to Laura's face from behind and she collapsed into his arms. Winston took Laura away leaving Evie hysterical and crying her eyes out upstairs. Laura was dying and there was nothing Evie could do about it, but she knew who had sent Winston and she knew her mummy was not the last person Winston was coming for. Evie's enhanced gut instinct knew who had sent Winston; it was Death itself! Laura was not supposed to be alive as she had cheated Death by not drowning that day by the river after I warned her. Death had come to reclaim her. It didn't seem to be any consolation whatsoever Laura was going to live again in the New Order, she was going to get a second chance of life. God is merciful, God loves us. Most previous transgressions get wiped clean; we all start again. Laura would have another chance to adapt to the New Order but would she meet me there again?

The biggest ramification now was Evie had lost her mummy. There was only one place she was heading and that was to my place. Evie was heading to El Campo, but how?

I was alone in my house still feeling very sad and lonely having lost Amy Jane. It was around 9 p.m. at night and I had retired for the evening to my bedroom when I could hear crying. It sounded like a little girl crying.

"Evie, is that you? Why are you crying?" I asked this little girl, feeling really concerned and worried as Evie's distress had made itself known in my mind. Evie wanted her daddy and I was her daddy so I could pick up her distress as she directed it at me.

"Daddy, mummy's gone," cried Evie.

"What do you mean, mummy's gone?" I asked her, now feeling a real trepidation.

"The bad man took her away," cried Evie.

"What bad man?" I asked, now really feeling my sense of dread.

"Death took her, daddy. Death took my mummy away. Can I come to live with you, daddy? I need you, daddy," cried Evie.

"Of course you can," I said, feeling very concerned but highly traumatised. "Stay there; don't leave the house. I'll be coming straight down to pick you up; it will take me 3 hours to get to you by car so please be patient, Evie. I am coming, daddy's coming."

"But daddy, you don't need to drive. I can come to you, can I? Can I? Please, daddy!" pleaded Evie.

"Of course you can, but how?" I asked her, feeling so confused.

"Daddy, just think about your house. Think about where you live and I will see it, daddy. I will come," said Evie.

I concentrated very hard in my mind, focusing on my house, picturing it in my mind and then she was here; Evie was here! "Evie, how did you get here? What the .....! What's going on? I don't understand; this is like some kind of strange magic. Are you alright, Evie?" I said, nearly fainting with shock.

Evie just ran into my arms and hugged me for all it was worth. She had brought her favourite doll and favourite teddy bear with her. Evie was here to stay with me for sure. I had just been given evidence, startling evidence, that Evie was not only my little girl, she was my very special little girl. She seemed to have extraordinary powers. She could communicate by thought and she could teleport. Evie had a perfect body; she was a product of another world, a world that was only supposed to be available to a person when they die or survive the last days. Evie was just a young girl for now but as she grew up she would become even more important to me. I had lost my dad, I had lost Amy Jane to another man called Bradley and now I had lost Laura, my New Order sweetheart. Despite the wonderful Evie, a lot of my world seemed like it was caving in. I hadn't yet realised Evie's presence in this world had made it a totally different world to how it was supposed to be. Just how different was it?

CHAPTER 11

GETTING TO KNOW
MY LITTLE GIRL

April 2006

"Daddy! Daddy! Where are you taking me today?" asked Evie in such a joyful and enthusiastic way that only a little girl could express with such innocence and charm.

"I thought I would take you to the zoo," I replied. "Shall we go to the zoo? Would you like that?"

"Yes, daddy!" beamed Evie as she jumped up and down in excitement. "Let's go to the zoo." Evie loved animals and she had let me know in no uncertain terms what she thought of me when I used to tuck into my full English breakfast. She would burst into hysterical tears as she berated me.

"Daddy, you're eating an animal. Please stop it, daddy; it is not right. Please stop it, daddy. I don't like this!"

I could see how distressed she was. I had to reflect on what I was eating. "I'm sorry, princess. I didn't know just how much it hurt you to see me eating meat." I told her feeling very guilty.

"It is wrong, daddy. Animals are our friends. Please don't eat them, daddy. It is wrong for animals to be hurt; it is so wrong, daddy," cried Evie.

"I won't eat meat from now on, princess," I said.

"Thank you, daddy," replied Evie.

It had certainly given me more food for thought as I realised everybody in the New Order was Vegan and reminded me of the special bond that was created between humans and animals in the New Order. I had to bear in mind Evie was a natural extension of this and the trip to the zoo was going to give me another eye opener to Evie's powers.

"Which animals would you like to see first, Evie?" I asked her.

"The monkeys, daddy. I would like to go and see the monkeys," answered Evie.

As we approached the general area of the monkeys' enclosure, it was very apparent they were making an almighty din with their screeching and boisterousness. They were so full of energy as they swung from and climbed anything they could find, but as soon as they saw Evie all the monkeys just stopped in their tracks. They became becalmed as they just stood there, entranced with Evie and it was enough to get her crying.

"I don't like this," she cried.

"What's the matter, princess?" I asked her. "What's wrong?"

"I don't like the monkeys being caged, daddy," cried Evie. "They shouldn't be trapped; they should be free. It's not right; I don't like this."

"But lots of people love the monkeys," I told her. "The monkeys can be funny and entertaining. They give pleasure to lots of little boys and girls who wouldn't see them otherwise."

"Monkeys are supposed to be free, daddy. All the animals are supposed to be free," said Evie. "Animals are our friends."

"You couldn't let all the animals run free," I said. "Some are very dangerous to humans."

"Which animals, Daddy?" asked Evie.

"Definitely the lions and the tigers." I answered. "They would most likely kill us if they got hold of us."

"I am not scared of lions and tigers, daddy," protested Evie. "They are our friends. They wouldn't hurt us."

"I think I will beg to differ with you on that one," I argued. "I wouldn't want to try and find out if a lion would hurt me or not as I am pretty sure I would be a dead man if I did."

"Don't worry, daddy. They are cuddly," said Evie, urging me to take her to see the lions.

"There they are," I said as we approached their cage. "Just look at them; they are anything but cuddly. Don't go too near the fence, Evie. They are very dangerous."

"Daddy, they're coming over. I want to stroke one." Said Evie.

"You can't stroke a lion," I shouted. "It will rip your hand off," I said, but couldn't help noticing the lions were like in a trance.

"Look, daddy, they want to be stroked. I told you they would," said Evie. "I will show you."

"Please don't go near the fence, Evie, we will all be in trouble," I shouted. "Please come away now."

"Daddy, you need to trust me," cried Evie, as she slipped from my grasp and proceeded to put her hand through the fence. I went numb with shock and was just about to go into panic mode.

"Look daddy, he loves me. The lion is licking my hand. I told you it is not dangerous. It wants you to stroke him. He is tilting his head for you. Are you going to stroke him, daddy?"

"Er ....., er ..... I am not sure. I don't think it's wise," I told her.

"You're not scared, are you, daddy?" laughed Evie. "I told you, daddy. Lions are our friends. They won't hurt you, daddy, they want to be loved."

I still didn't have the courage to answer Evie's challenge as I definitely didn't think I had the calming powers she possessed as Evie was a very special girl. She was not of this world. I was just a mere mortal compared to her. Evie had seen enough of the zoo to know it was not a place she wanted to come back to in a hurry, It upset her too much. I was certainly learning some very big lessons when it came to Evie.

It was clear that Evie had settled in really well with her new family after the terrible events surrounding her mum, Laura. As Evie approached her 5th birthday and beyond, she had taken a shine to all my loved ones. I had a rival for Evie's affections and that was my mum. Evie loved to call her Nanny Pat and Nanny Pat, my mum, had just found a new fella. His name was Ewan and he was a God's onlooker just like mum. In fact, Ewan was an Elder. I liked him; he was a nice man, a gentle and meek man. Mum had chosen well. I liked Ewan's wisdom; I thought he was a nice man. Ewan the Wise did have a ring to it. Mum and Ewan had even held hands, so I knew it was serious. Their convictions that we were living in the last days were stronger than ever. Mum was urging me to join up to save myself and Evie was getting old enough to really identify with what mum was preaching as she was always talking about the good news of God's New Order. Evie knew it was all true; she was living proof of that. Evie loved Nanny Pat's faith in what was to come. She was only a little girl for now but knew just how much Nanny Pat loved God. Evie loved Nanny Pat and her beloved dog, Freddie, a Yorkshire cross.

Evie had also met my son, Dean and was in awe of him. She loved his bravado and seeing him in his army uniform. Dean was her half-brother and she couldn't have been more proud of him knowing how brave he was, although she knew she wanted him to be at home more often. She wanted to play with her big brother.

There was also her two cousins, Jodie and Lollypop. Evie was going to start school with Jodie in her class. Jodie was a member of God's onlookers just like Nanny Pat but she was only a little girl, just like Evie. Jodie was a vulnerable little girl and Evie, in time, was going to be Jodie's champion as she looked after family and a future fellow onlooker. Lollypop was a year younger than Evie but would also need her help in the future as school would prove to be a real battleground for them in the future, a case of three girls growing up together in a very challenging environment.

Evie had been accepted by one and all and had been embraced but she shouldn't be here and I, in time, was going to find more devastating consequences. What were they?

December 2009

Evie had now been living with me for over 4 years. She was a special daughter and had remained diligent in not standing out, despite her special differences. Evie was growing up normally, unimpeded by her gifts and that was the way she wanted it. Evie had chosen to follow Nanny Pat into the God's Onlookers and was not particularly bothered about the coming Christmas as they didn't celebrate Christmas, but the one thing she loved about Christmas was my son, Dean, her half-brother, coming home from army leave for a much-needed break from serving in war-torn Iraq, another thing that my mum had mentioned to me in the New Order that had seemed to come true with the rise of the Islamic militants.

I could see how bad the world was; it seemed to be much worse than described by my mum. The planet was already warming up alarmingly and the wickedness of so many people seemed overwhelming already. I was very worried about Dean fighting a war abroad; I was so looking forward to seeing him. I couldn't help thinking unsettled thoughts that this was not how it was supposed to be. It shouldn't be like this, at least not yet that the world around me was different to what my mum described to me in the New Order and then the penny dropped; she had obviously never mentioned Evie in her descriptions of what happened, as Evie hadn't existed then. This world was different because of Evie's presence. She had unwittingly changed all the dynamics of time. A person from the New Order shouldn't be in this world and everything seemed to be up in the air now and being rewritten. History was being changed from its original design, but in what way? For better or worse? It did, unfortunately, seem the latter. In Dean's case, I distinctly remembered my mum mentioning that Dean spent only a short time in the army before leaving it and then something hit me straight in the eyes as I recalled something else. Dean actually admitted to me in the New Order when he spoke to me there that he started seeing Amy Jane in 2008 and married her in 2010. It was me that was the fly in the ointment; it was my survival from that car accident that had changed history. I was the cause of how the world was different. Was I always supposed to be dead? Was I always supposed to die that day? It was not Evie; it was me behind all the chaos. Did Evie know this? How could all this be resolved?

A sign of everything spinning out of control was sitting down with Evie watching Britain's Got Skill and Evie suddenly said, "Dad, you see that man judging the acts? He is going to be in charge of the country soon."

"What? Simon? Do you think it can really happen? I think he is far too busy and making so much money to want the hassle. There is the X Feature; it is far too successful for him to want to swap, but I could imagine he would like the power," I commented.

"No, not Simon, dad; that other man on the other side," Evie told me.

"You mean Fierce Morgan. Oh my God! I hope you're wrong," I replied. "He is incredibly opinionated and sure of himself."

"He is going to be Prime Minister in the next couple of years, I have a really strong feeling and he is going to be the most divisive Prime Minister in history.

He is going to change this country beyond recognition." Said Evie.

"I so hope you're wrong, Evie, but I doubt you are," I told her. "I have to ask you, how do you know such things? You have such an amazing sixth sense; you seem too special for this world. I love you dearly, Evie, but are you aware why you are here? You have gifts of the New Order that nobody else has. We are all imperfect in this world except you. I am so glad I am your dad and so proud of you, but do you have a strong sense of self? What do you want to do in this world? Do you know yet?"

"I am only 8 years old, dad, but I do know I am here for you," answered Evie, "but I am only a young girl now. I want to have the same fun as Jodie and Lollypop; I want to enjoy growing up into being a young woman and enjoy the human experience. I love going to school; Jodie is so clever, so intelligent and always comes top of the class. It makes her so happy; she is almost like a genius for her age but I do let her come top, dad. I could beat her if I wanted to as the school work is far too easy for me but I don't want to stand out, I don't want to be noticed. I look out for Jodie as she is one of God's Onlookers; she is so brave. I do think you should become one of God's Onlookers, dad. Nanny Pat is one and her husband Ewan. They are Onlookers, so why not get to know why they are so passionate about what they believe in?"

"I might go one day. I will think about it," I told Evie.

"You should, dad," urged Evie, "because they are right. God is coming. You don't want to be on the wrong side."

"I know, Evie. Nanny Pat told me all about it in the New Order. I know I have to change and be a better person," I said.

"You are a good person, dad. I love you, dad. I am so happy to be your daughter. The New Order is real; I want us all to be alive in the New Order all together," revealed Evie.

"So do I, Evie. So do I," I agreed.

That was such a heavy conversation I had with my delightful daughter. I was beginning to really get to know my girl now. Evie was still very young but already aware of the bigger picture. She was special but she didn't want to stand out as special. She was humble, such an important quality to have. Evie could outshine anybody, even Jodie, but she chose not to. Evie was humble; she wanted to enjoy her life in this world, unhindered by an excessive show of what she was really capable of. Evie was wise beyond her years; she loved living in the moment of being a young girl, going to school, going swimming with Jodie and Lollypop and being a pain in the neck to her half-brother, Dean. He had come home to visit on army leave and it was beautiful to see him again after such a prolonged time away. I was so proud of my son and Evie almost hero-worshipped him like some sort of celebrity; that was until the day came he had to leave us again and Evie just burst into hysterical tears.

"Dean must not go back to Iraq" she cried. "He must not go."

"I know, Evie," I sympathised. "I don't want him to go either, but he has to. He is serving his country. I hate it when he is away but what can you do? I know you love your brother."

"You don't understand, dad; he must not go back," cried Evie. "The bad man is back; Winston is back."

"Bad man? The last time you mentioned a bad man was when your mum went away. Are you saying he is coming for Dean?" I asked her, paralysed with panic.

"Yes, dad. He is coming. He is in Iraq already. He is waiting for him. You have to talk to Dean; you have to stop him going. His life is in danger," warned Evie hysterically. "Dean is going to die."

"I am going to, Evie. I believe you," I replied, as I sought out my son who was now back in full military uniform.

"Dean, can I have a word, son?"

"What's that, dad? I have to be going; I can't miss my pick-up or I will be in big trouble," replied Dean.

"You can't go, son. You must stay," I pleaded with him.

"You're having a laugh, aren't you, dad?" said Dean. "Do you know what the army would do if I didn't go back? It doesn't need explaining. I have to go. I am not a deserter; it is the biggest sin there is. Why don't you want me to go?"

"Your life is in danger, Dean. I don't want you to go. I love you too much. I do not want to lose you," I pleaded.

"I know my life is in danger there, dad. Iraq is a nutty place but I am a soldier; I have been trained for combat. My life is in danger every day I am there, but this is what I devoted my life for. Why are you acting so strange, dad? You have never been like this before when I have had to go back to Afghanistan or Iraq," asked Dean.

"Evie thinks you are in big danger, son," I told him. "You have to take this seriously."

"Are you for real?" Dean questioned me incredulously. "Are you seriously expecting me to say I can't go back? They will ask me why and I tell them it's because my 8 year old half-sister said I could die. I would be laughed at and ridiculed by my peers for all my life. I am sorry, I have to go."

"Dean, Evie says you're going to die," I warned him. "Evie knows things we don't. You have to believe her."

"I am going now, dad. I hope you are better when I next see you."

Evie ran to the door, crying. "Dean, please don't go. Please stay. I love you, Dean. I beg you, please don't go." Evie was in hysterics. She loved her big brother.

Dean was wrong; he wasn't going to see us again. On the 18th March 2010 there was the most dreaded knock on my door.

"Is this Paul Jackson?"

"Yes, this is me," I replied.

"Can we come in? We have some bad news," they replied solemnly.

"Oh my God! I know what you're going to say. Dean is dead, isn't he?" I wailed in distress. "This is unbearable; I can't stand this. Are you telling me my son is dead?"

"We are sorry to tell you, Mr Jackson, that your son has died in action. He was a very brave man; your son was a hero. I know that's not any consolation at this time but your son died doing his duty, doing what he loved," they told me.

"My son, my beautiful son!! He was only 23 years old," I screamed. "That's such a short life. It is not fair; I can't stand this! Why Dean? Why did it have to be Dean? I do not know what I am going to do without him. This is too much to bear. How did it happen? How? How?"

"Please try to calm down, Mr Jackson," they pleaded with me. "Please take some deep breaths. Try to breathe. You son is a hero; he died saving others. It was a tragic accident; it could have happened to anyone. It was just bad luck."

"What was bad luck?" I asked them.

"It was friendly fire. Dean was in the wrong place at the wrong time. There will be an Inquiry," they told me.

"Private Winston is distraught; it was such a tragic accident."

"Winston? Did you say Winston?" I said, feeing rigid with shock.

"We have already told you more than we should, Mr. Jackson," they replied. "I am afraid we can't divulge anymore information. I am sure it was all a tragic accident. Are you going to be alright? Mr Jackson? Do you have anyone with you?"

"I have my young daughter, Evie," I answered.

"Is that enough?" they asked. "Do you want someone to stay with you?"

"No thanks," I said, before shutting the door. My life felt like it was in ruins. My world felt like it was falling apart. I thanked God for my mum and family and I thanked God for Evie. That's all it seemed I had. Evie knew what was coming; she knew a bad man was coming back; she knew Dean was in great peril. She did her best to warn us. Would this bad man come back again? Who was this mysterious Winston? I needed another conversation with my daughter, but it would have to wait until after my son's funeral. I couldn't cope with my loss; I had to wait for my grief to subside as the next few weeks were hell.

This incident was the straw that broke the camel's back. I was going to fully re-evaluate my life; I was going to be an Onlooker just like Evie and my mum, her Nanny Pat. I had nothing much else; I was a single man and couldn't see that changing. I had lost Amy Jane and I had lost Laura. How I missed Amy Jane. I wondered how she was. How I wished I had her love right now, but I hadn't. I truly hoped she was happy because I wasn't. I wondered if she had truly found love with Bradley.

It took a few weeks before I felt well enough to have an important conversation with my daughter. Evie had also taken Dean's death really badly. She was just an 8 year old girl after all. Evie was finding that having perfection didn't insulate her from the overwhelming emotions a girl possesses, not in this world. Evie had cried her eyes out over Dean; she did not want him to die. It was a part of the human experience that Evie was not prepared for and she was going to find out as she grew older that feminine hormones were so tricky. They were not to be messed with and that they could test even the most perfect of people. Evie was going to find being a young girl was anything but easy! It could be the new hell! She didn't know what was coming; she had no idea!

In the meantime, I needed that conversation with Evie. What did she know? It was time to find out.

"Evie, can we talk, princess?" I asked her.

"Yes, dad. I am ready," said Evie.

"How do you know so much about this bad man? You know his name in Winston. I really need to know how you know so much, and how you know when he is coming." I asked her.

"I feel his presence in this world when he comes. I can just feel this terrible premonition that he is around. He is not here all the time; he comes and goes, but he is evil; he is a bad man. He has been sent by Death itself; he is death. Winston is a bad man; we must avoid him. He is clever; he can reinvent himself into anything. He was a boiler man when he took mummy and a soldier when he took Dean. He will come again; Winston will come again, but as what I don't know."

"Oh my God! This is terrible," I replied. "I wonder who he will come for next? I am scared, Evie. Why does he keep coming?"

"It's you, daddy. It's because of you he keeps coming back, I won't let him harm you. I know when he is coming; I will warn you. We will escape but you have to listen to me however strange it might sound. I can protect you." Said Evie.

"But why is the bad man angry with me? What have I done to deserve this? Do you know, Evie?" I asked her.

"You cheated death, dad. You should be dead, but I am so glad you are not. You should have died in that road accident and you came back to life. Death had you and you came back; Death felt cheated. It wants what it feels is his. It was the same with my mummy, Laura. She cheated Death until it came back for her. Death is especially angry with you as you warned her, so it wants to make you suffer," said Evie. "That is why Dean is dead; you are being punished mercilessly until it gets you, but Dean will live again in the New Order; you can meet him again."

"I hate myself. I am responsible; I don't want to live if other people suffer. I need to surrender myself," I cried.

"I don't want you to," said Evie. "I love you as my dad. I want us to live," pleaded Evie. "We will find a way to overcome the bad man. You must go to the Onlookers now. They are guided by God's Word. They will help protect you as well and we will pray for the others. I don't want to scare you, dad, but the bad man has not gone away. I can still sense him. I don't know what he is up to yet, but I don't sense he is coming for you."

"I really don't like the sound of this, Evie," I quivered, before hearing the postman deliver some letters. There was a very special letter from Amy Jane; wow! Amy Jane had sent me a letter. I was so excited to read it; it said,

> *"Dear Paul, I hope you are well. I had to write to you as I just heard about Dean and I am so sorry. He was a lovely young lad; I am devastated. I am thinking of you so much; I do miss you, Paul. I loved you but have moved on now. Bradley and I are happy; we are going on a very special adventure, a European Rail adventure soon. We are flying to Istanbul and making our way back by train. I hope Evie is making you smile. I do not bear any grudges, Paul; you did the right thing – she is your daughter. I hope in time I can come and see you both together. Time is a great healer, isn't it? With love, from Amy Jane."*

"That was beautiful. That was so nice of her to write to me," I said, starting to cry. "I miss her, Evie. I really do."

"Don't cry, dad," comforted Evie. "I don't like seeing you cry; I hate seeing you sad.

"I am sorry, princess," I replied. "Some things are really hard to get over, I guess."

"It is okay, dad," said Evie, before wincing and recoiling in terror. "Oh no, I can sense the bad man again."

"Oh No!" I cried. "Where? Where is he?"

"I can sense he is in a pilot's uniform. Oh no! Your Amy Jane is in trouble. He is coming for Amy Jane," shrieked Evie.

"We have to warn her immediately but she didn't leave a contact number or address. Oh my God! What can we do?" I said, feeling panic in the pits of my stomach.

"I can do it," said Evie. "If you have a photo of her, I can contact her by thought. I can do this but it will probably freak her out. It will make her realise I can do something that is out of this world, but what else can we do? I could teleport but that would be too much for her. I will try thought transfer; I hope it will be enough."

"Go ahead, Evie. I don't care what she would think; I need her to listen to you. I am desperate, Evie. Please go ahead," I pleaded with her.

"Here goes, dad," said Evie. "I can see her photo. I am concentrating; I am reaching her mind now. She is so confused; I am saying 'Amy Jane, please listen to me.

I am Evie. You have to listen; there is a bad man coming for you'. Amy Jane is not responding. She thinks she is going mad. This is so frustrating. It is the most natural thing in the world to think to each other," stressed Evie. "I do not think she is taking any notice of me. Oh no!"

"What do you mean oh no?" I asked her with dread.

"Amy Jane is already on the plane. I have heard the intercom say that Winston is their pilot and he hopes they all have a safe and pleasant journey. Oh no, it's too late. Her boyfriend, Bradley, is with her. They have no idea!! Oh no!" shrieked Evie.

The news that night made very grim reading. There had been a plane accident on landing in Istanbul. There had been two fatalities, two very unfortunate souls that had been seated closest to the right wing, a Bradley Beddingfield and an Amy Jane Wainfleet. My Amy Jane had gone. It was horror upon horror upon horror. I couldn't take all this; I wanted to die. Death would be merciful in the circumstances. It would be a release from this personal hell on Earth.

I couldn't even be placated by Evie telling me the bad man had gone. Winston had gone for now but we knew he would return. Where and when and how? And even more importantly, who for?

CHAPTER 12

FATAL DISTRACTION

January 2014

It had been over 3 years since that terrible period of my life where I lost my son and my true love, and it had been such a welcome relief that there had been no sign of the bad man coming back. Perhaps he had done his worst, as he had seen he had broken me and also, he knew I was suffering terribly in this world around me.

Evie's prediction about Fierce Morgan had come true and it had made my world even more bleak. Fierce Morgan had recently been made Prime Minister on a Common Sense Mandate with his Common Sense Party and was already making his mark on the country. To make things worse, Evie had told me that in 2016 there was going to be the perfect storm when the Donald became USA President, when a clash of two gigantic egos would collide; the world was indeed in great peril. The 'fierce one' had already affected my love of Premier Leage football. He had made it illegal for any team to beat his beloved Arsenal so no team could stop them being champions. He gave a compulsory relegation to Spurs, Liverpool and Manchester United, plus Manchester City on alleged corruption charges. He also had made Kevin

Peters, a brilliantly talented cricketer but divisive character, his Foreign Secretary and Ambassador to the United Nations.

The 'fierce one' didn't give a monkeys what people thought, but they seemed to like him. His monstrous ego was out of control. He wrote a book and made it law that everybody bought it, so he was naturally the biggest author around and then bragged mercilessly how he was so brilliant. His opinion, and his opinion alone, was sacrosanct. Fierce Morgan was a very scary man, perhaps even more than the bad man himself. He took no prisoners, and he took fools very badly. In 2013 he had Bumbling Boris jailed for alleged cowardice. He had disbanded the Houses of Parliament and moved Government to a television studio in London and was appointing friends into very high places; some would call it cronyism, but hasn't that always been the case? Susanah Reeves was made Home Secretary, Samantha Holden was made the Secretary for Sexy Women, Bear Willis was made Defence Secretary and Simon de Cruel was made the Chancellor as he had more money than the country put together allegedly. Craig Really Horrid was moved from Strictly to Minister for the Dark Arts. Fierce Morgan's effect on the country was transformational, but the serious stuff was still to come in due course.

None of this had any effect on Evie; she was now 12½ years old and in Year 8 at senior school. Jodie was in her year also and Lollypop was in the year below. Up until now it was only the bad man that had kept Evie awake at night, but he hadn't stirred for ages and maybe Evie had allowed herself to become a little bit complacent as she was now fully involved and immersed in school life and in the delights of being a teenager. Evie was to discover her body, her changing body, was going to give her more problems and more challenges than any bad man. The remorseless march of feminine hormones and the puberty inside her was going to test her like nothing else on Earth! She was going to discover having perfection didn't give you a vaccine when it came to being a female teenager.

Evie and Jodie and Lollypop were passionate God's Onlookers and Nanny Pat in particular was extremely proud of all three. They shared her total faith that God was coming as did I, although not at their level. It seemed nothing could get in the way of this, but Evie, in particular, was going to have the test of her life and that was boys! They were all going to get tested like never before!

There was one big difference between them though. Evie would not have to suffer periods. Evie's reproduction system had been rendered inert. It was one of the blessings, the many blessings Evie enjoyed having this perfect body. She wasn't designed to be on this Earth to have a baby; this was not her purpose. Evie was here to be my guide. Evie was the girl that didn't have periods and how all the girls would prove to be so jealous of her as they fought their monthly battles!

Evie had blossomed into a very beautiful young girl, with all the prettiness and developing attributes that young femininity brings. It was like she was changing into a young lady very quickly as her natural assets bloomed, and while she could avoid the biggest curse of femininity that would mean the dreaded time of the month, it hadn't stopped those formidable and pesky feminine hormones running amok and out of control inside her. Evie dearly wished they weren't so powerful as they were bombarding her with what they found attractive ..... boys!!

Evie hadn't given any boy a minute's attention, but now her hormones were hammering on her mind's door. The perceived delights of boys was going to distract Evie away from what was important in her life – God's Onlookers and me! It was so natural for a beautiful young girl to want to be desired as such, to be embraced, to have a feeling of being in love and being loved in return, albeit in an innocent way. The biggest consequence of not having to go through the dreaded part of the menstrual cycle was Evie forever being in the goldilocks zone, where oestrogen and progesterone were in perfect balance. It was like Evie was in the phantom ovulation part of the cycle where a girl feels so good about herself and so confident about herself and even just a little bit sexy. Evie's hormones were indeed her ultimate adversary and it didn't take long before perfect Evie was totally in their grip, and it came in the name of Eamonn Rafferty!

Eamonn Rafferty was a young Irish charmer, and he was captain of the school's football team at under 13 level. He played like a young George Best, full of beguiling flair with his ball playing trickery and skill. When he wasn't in his school uniform, Eamonn could be seen in his distinctive green and white hooped Celtic top. It wasn't Evie that first noticed Eamonn's charm; it was her younger cousin, Lollypop, in the year below. Lollypop had become smitten with this young Irish charmer who had oodles and oodles of charisma and laddish charm, so much so that Lollypop had suddenly become a fully paid-up fan of the school football team. It was so out of character as Lollypop, as well as Evie and her older sister Jodie had always hated football, so to suddenly be so interested could only be down to one thing. Lollypop was younger than Evie and Jodie, but it had seemed her own pesky feminine hormones had kicked in earlier than them. Eamonn Rafferty was the reason behind Lollypop's sudden reborn eagerness to embrace something she hated; Eamonn Rafferty was the only reason!

Lollypop started walking around like she had her head in the clouds dreaming about this young Irish stud, and it hadn't gone unnoticed as it began clouding her enthusiasm for the Onlookers. The Onlookers saw themselves as akin to the Righteous Class in the New Order. They didn't encourage mixing with what they deemed Unrighteous people, so they were very concerned that Lollypop was wavering. Lollypop needed a chaperone, and who was better than the perfect Evie, her cousin. Evie was not very pleased, as Lollypop wanted to go and see the school's football team play another school in the cup final. Eamonn Rafferty was playing; he was captain, he was like a young Irish Jack Grealish! Lollypop was so excited; she dolled herself up to the nines. She had her favourite lipstick on, as who knows, it might have come in useful as Lollypop dreamed of Eamonn kissing her on the lips. How bad would that go with the Onlookers, as kissing was definitely unbecoming outside marriage. Holding hands was as far as you could go, but Lollypop dreamed of more. She needed reigning in and Evie was the girl needed to do it.

"Oh, Evie! I am so excited about tonight," said Lollypop as she applied her last bit of make-up, It had taken three hours. "Thank you so much for coming with me. I can't wait to see Eamonn play tonight."

"I am not looking forward to it," protested Evie. "Football is a silly game; it is a stupid game. I don't know how anybody stands it. It is so boring seeing a silly ball being kicked around."

"I know," admitted Lollypop. "But Eamonn is there; he will be in his shorts. He will be showing off his manly legs. Have you heard him talk? His Irish accent can melt any girl's heart. Eamonn is a stud muffin and I want him to be my Irish stud muffin."

"Oh, Lollypop, you are being so silly. No boy is worthy of all this sickly talk. You do know you are being sidetracked from what is important; you know the world is in trouble and you are just walking around like you are in a trance," counselled Evie. "Just fight it; it is only a silly phase. You will snap out of it."

"Evie, you don't understand," argued Lollypop. "I love him; I love Eamonn Rafferty."

"Oh, come on," said a dismissive Evie, who hadn't yet realised how delicate and precarious a young girl's heart operated. It was almost like it didn't have blood pumping around it; it had treacle pumping around it instead. Evie was a perfect girl; she didn't know, did she? She couldn't know, could she? How could she know?

"I do love him, I do," argued Lollypop. "Please don't show me up, Evie. Oh look, there is that girl in your class over there. It is Jessie Johnson."

"Oh no," said Evie, hoping Jessie wouldn't notice them. It was too late.

"Fancy seeing you two here," said Jessie. "I never thought I would see the day you two were at a football match. I wonder why?" she teased.

"We like football. What's wrong with that?" protested Lollypop. "Are you here watching your boyfriend, Samuel? He is the goalkeeper, isn't he?"

"Yes, he is," confirmed Jessie. "Are you here to watch anybody? I bet you are, aren't you? Go on, tell me; you can tell me. Is it Aaron or is it Eamonn? It is so Eamonn, isn't it? You are blushing, Lollypop, I can see it. You are here to see Eamonn, aren't you?"

"I am not blushing," protested Lollypop. "Please go away, you are upsetting me. I am not here to see Eamonn."

"Yes, please go away, Jessie," said Evie. "Lollypop loves football; She is not here for any stupid boy. Boys are silly creatures; they are not mature enough for us, so we are here for the football and the football only."

"I can believe you are not here for any boy, Evie," replied Jessie, "but Lollypop certainly is. I can see it in her face. If you like football, Lollypop, tell me one famous footballer. I bet you can't, can you?"

"Em ....., em ..... maybe I can't, but that doesn't mean I don't like football. I love football," said a flustered Lollypop.

"Yeah, right," mocked Jessie, "and I am the Queen Mary. I thought it was more important for you two to be knocking on people's doors; you are God's Onlookers, aren't you?" I've seen you in action so I can't understand why you are here unless Lollypop is in love."

"I'm telling you, Jessie, I'm not," cried Lollypop. "I don't like this, Evie, can we leave?"

"Don't let Jessie bully you," said a determined Evie. "We are staying right here. We don't get bullied by anybody; we are Onlookers and we are proud. We are having no girl telling us why or why not we can be here. Go away, Jessie."

"Yes, go away, Jessie," said Lollypop. "Thank you, Evie. You told her, didn't you?

Evie was proud she had stuck up for Lollypop, but what had she done? She could be on the way home now, not stuck at this wretched football match. Lollypop was gazing longingly at this dreamboat playing on their side of the pitch, admiring him so much as he beat his opponents with his sublime skills. His charming flair was there for all to see.

"Oh my God, he is such a dreamboat," drooled Lollypop. "I love him."

"Lollypop, you're drooling," said Evie.

"I am so not," argued Lollypop.

Evie was about to agree to disagree with her cousin when Eamonn Rafferty looked over at her and flashed his charming and roguish smile at her, completely freezing her in her tracks.

"What is the matter, Evie? You have gone quiet. Did you see Eamonn look over at us? I am sure he was smiling at us. He is such a sortie; I would like him to sort me," said Lollypop.

"You're not to say that, Lollypop," admonished Evie, before again seeing her gaze freeze upon the footballing adonis that was Eamonn Rafferty.

"Evie? Evie? You were daydreaming; you just stood there open-mouthed. What are you looking at? Evie, can you hear me? You are not eyeing up Eamonn, are you? How could you? You are supposed to be supporting me, not competing with me. Will you stop staring at hunky Eamonn," shouted Lollypop.

"I am so sorry, Lollypop," realised a very shocked and very bashful Evie. "I don't know what came over me. This is not supposed to happen to me. I feel so ashamed; I am so sorry, Lollypop. Please forgive me."

"Do you fancy my Eamonn?" said Lollypop.

"Of course not; don't be silly. I am much too disciplined for any of that nonsense," replied Evie.

"So why were you staring at him like a long-lost puppy? I saw you and I don't like it. I want us to go now," cried Lollypop.

With that rebuke from a very miffed Lollypop, they both left. Evie felt terrible; what on Earth was she doing? How could she be like that? How could she upset Lollypop so much? Evie was so confused, especially as that night she couldn't get Eamonn out of her mind however hard she tried. Evie was smitten; her treacherous hormones had shown their devious hand and the next day Eamonn Rafferty came over to her.

"Hello, Evie. Did you enjoy the football match last night? We won 3-2 and I got the winner, but you had gone by then. I couldn't help noticing you as you are such a pretty girl. I smiled at you because I liked you; do you like me? I saw you looking at me so I did wonder."

"I ....., I ....., I wasn't looking at you; I was looking at the football," protested a very flustered Evie. Where was her perfection when she needed it? She had lost clarity of thought and in a rush to clear herself of her humiliation, she implicated Lollypop. "I was there for Lollypop. She is crazy about you."

"That's nice," dismissed Eamonn. "She is a nice girl but it was you I was smiling at and you didn't look away. You like me, don't you, Evie?"

"I do not!" replied an irked Evie, clearly unsettled with Eamon's bravado and arrogance.

"You do, Evie. I saw the way you looked at me. You like me," teased Eamonn. "You like me, don't you?"

"You seem very cocksure of yourself, don't you, Eamonn?" Evie answered.

"I know; I am worth it," was his arrogant reply, "But I like you, Evie. I would like to be your boyfriend. Would you like to be my girlfriend?"

"Er ....., er ....., I'm not sure," stuttered Evie as she fought her urge to say yes please. What was happening to her? How come she couldn't control her damn hormones?

"What's stopping you saying yes?" asked Eamonn. "Wouldn't you like to go out with me?"

"It is not that you are not good looking; you are, by goodness, you are so hot," replied Evie, now beside herself with disgust at herself. Was she feeling lust? Surely not.

"Why, then? Give me one good reason, Evie," encouraged Eamonn.

"I'm one of God's Onlookers. We are Righteous; we are supposed to keep ourselves to ourselves. We aren't supposed to mix. I am sorry, Eamonn, I can't see you. The Elders will be furious with me," said Evie, feeling like she was going to cry.

"I understand," said Eamonn. "What you are saying is I am not good enough for you. I understand. I tell you what; I will give you a week to say yes to me and if you don't, I will move on. I have been asked out by three other girls, but it was you I wanted. If you haven't said yes to me in a week, you have lost me for good. I don't give girls second chances."

Evie tried to be strong, she really did, but Eamonn was in her head; Eamonn was in her heart. Evie gave in and Lollypop was furious; she would not talk to Evie for months. All Evie could think about was Eamonn and being in his arms. It felt so wrong as all her instincts were telling her to stop it, but her heart was ruling her head so it felt so right. Evie and Eamonn were now an item and it had created a great chasm in her relationships with her family and the Onlookers, including her beloved Nanny Pat. Eamonn was making her forget about her dearest ones, including me, as she fell more and more under his spell and Eamonn was ready to up the ante.

"I love you, Evie. We have been going out for three months now. Are you ready for a snog? Would you like a nice kiss and cuddle, Evie? Do you want me to kiss you?" asked Eamonn.

"I can't; I mustn't," replied Evie.

"Why not?" asked Eamonn. "You're even funny when I hold your hand."

"It is serious," said Evie. "Kissing someone is like you want to make a lifetime commitment to that person."

"Evie, you are longing to kiss me, I can see it in your eyes, and I long to kiss you as well" urged Eamonn.

"Please don't," protested Evie as his lips inched closer to hers before locking on. Evie could not resist as gentle kissing turned to passionate snogging. Evie was mortified; she was racked with guilt but she also felt exhilaration, so much exhilaration. Evie was floating on air.

"I told you that you would like that," said Eamonn. "Do you want to do it again?"

Evie did and she did it again and again and again. Evie was now lost in a sea of romance as her resistance yielded to its power. Evie's eyes were now well and truly off the ball; she only had eyes for Eamonn. Eamonn was her world now and Evie started removing herself from being in the Righteous Onlookers and it hadn't gone unnoticed by the Elders. Tony the Hawk had his eyes firmly locked on to her; nothing got past him as his sirens were blazing red. It was time to talk, time to counsel. It was time the Elders had a talk with her and it was Nanny Pat who was the person Evie most looked up to and could get to the bottom of what was going on.

"How are you, Evie?" said Tony the Hawk. "I have noticed, I mean all the Elders have noticed you are not as keen as you used to be. Is there anything troubling you? Us Elders are very concerned."

"No, I don't think so," answered Evie. "Why do you ask?"

"You've stopped spending time with your Nanny Pat and Jodie and Lollypop, You are not spending time with your dad. It is like your mind is elsewhere and your heart is elsewhere. Is there a reason for this?" asked Tony.

"I don't think so," answered Evie.

"But there is, isn't there?" commented Tony the Hawk. "I have spotted you with a boy and you were kissing him, weren't you? It is very wrong to mix with Unrighteous people, let alone kiss one. We are very disappointed with you. You need to seek urgent repentance or we will have to let you go."

Nanny Pat was distraught. "Oh Evie, how could you kiss a boy? You need to stop this. I know its hard being a teenage girl, it really is, but you have to respect the rules. I am so gutted."

"I'm sorry, Nanny Pat," replied Evie, "but I do love him. That is why we kiss."

"This conduct has to stop at once, Evie," warned Jefferson, another Elder watching in. "You have one warning; you need to comply if you want to remain Righteous and keep on the right spiritual path. You also need to repent; I can take care of that. You can get help."

Evie was about to say no thanks, when Nany Pat hit her with an Exocet missile. She had a secret to share with her, something Evie had overlooked in her being lost in lust with Eamonn. Evie normally had a brilliant sixth sense, but not this time, as Nanny Pat told her something she hadn't told me as she knew I would be very upset.

"Evie, I didn't want to tell you this yet, but I have bowel cancer. It is operable and I am hopeful everything will be fine but you can't be sure. You haven't spent much time with me lately, so I haven't had a chance to talk to you much. I thought it was important for you to know."

"I am so sorry," cried Evie. "I am so sorry. When are you going to hospital? I love you, Nanny; I will try to change."

"You need to," warned Jefferson. "Look at the world around you. It is in massive trouble. You don't have time to just follow your own selfish ways. You need to focus on your loved ones. I think this goes to show how important that is."

"I am a good person. There are plenty of good people in the world; they will be saved. I know there will be a war, but good people will survive, won't they?" remarked Evie.

"You are a good person," confirmed Jefferson, "but at the minute you are not Righteous. Good people will survive and good people will be born again, but it is only the Righteous that can lead. You know that, don't you? Everybody has to have a goal to be Righteous."

Evie had reached a very important crossroads in her young life. There was nothing stopping her carrying on with Eamonn, but it would come at a price. Evie's perfection was in peril; she was not acting in accordance to what she was here for and as she continued to be unable to resist the advances of Eamonn, she was going to get the shock of her life. She was going to get the most powerful warning yet that her body could lose its perfection status and her powers of the mind and this was to prove the ultimate fatal distraction as the bad man was coming back!

Despite her anguish over Nanny Pat, she didn't think Nanny Pat would not overcome it and she had relapsed into once again kissing and cuddling her boyfriend when it happened!, it was the most strangest of sensations to a startled Evie.

Evie felt different down below; what was happening? Evie was having her first period. Evie was the girl that didn't have periods but now she felt so yucky. Evie's body was losing its perfection as a price for her individual pursuits and she was beside herself with anxiety. Her once peaceful, calm and perceptive mind was anything but as she tried to absorb the significance.

Nanny Pat had gone into hospital for her bowel cancer operation and Evie's reducing mental status meant she didn't know; she just didn't realise Winston was back!

The operating surgeon on Nanny Pat was not called Winston by name, at least that was not his first name as Nanny Pat got rushed into theatre, but the anaesthetist was called Jamie, a Jamie Winston, and now, as

Nanny Pat lay on the operating table, he encouraged Nanny Pat:

> "Just count down from 10, Patricia. Inhale the anaesthetic in. You will be asleep in a couple of seconds. Night night and God bless!" The bad man had doubled the right dose of anaesthetic.

Nanny Pat never woke up again. She was another victim of the bad man and Evie had not cottoned onto it as her fatal distraction proved just that. Nanny Pat was dead; she was never supposed to be dead. Dean was never supposed to be dead. Amy Jane was never supposed to be dead, but they were. When would the bad man ever stop? He was remorseless; he was merciless and so hard to stop. He could be anything he wanted to be; a boiler man, a rogue soldier, a pilot and now an anaesthetist. What next?

When hearing the news, Evie dumped Eamonn in a heartbeat and sought immediate repentance with the Onlookers. Evie could not stand being just a normal person. It was scary seeing her perfection drained from her. Evie needed to reverse the decline; Evie needed to be sorry. She was, she truly was. It was just a shame it took the death of her beloved Nanny Pat to finally make her realise it!

The period of repentance was going to take time but Evie was serious; she wanted her perfect body and mind back. I needed her perfect body and mind back. The bad man was out there somewhere; was it my turn next?

It would take the best part of two years for Evie's perfection to return to her, and for her to regain her magical gifts again. Just what special and final plan did she have for me as my world caved in around me?

CHAPTER 13

IF I COULD TURN BACK TIME

December 2016

Eaton Mental Health Facility

"So, Paul, how are you today?" said the nurse. "Your daughter, Evie, is coming to see you soon. Are you ready for her visit, Mr. Jackson?"

I had been in the mental health facility ever since I heard about the death of my beloved mother. I couldn't take any more, the pain was too much for me to bear. I had tried to take my life but failed and I was rushed to this facility as an emergency, and it was only recently that I was feeling on the road to recovery. I had been a broken man and I couldn't care less if the bad man put me out of my misery, but true to his very cruel nature, he let me suffer just when I was ready to submit to him.

I had lost my mum, my son and my true love, plus Laura, the mum to my special daughter, Evie. How much more could any man take? I had seen Evie go off the rails at the wrong time. I know it's hard being a teenage girl; at least I can guess, but I was relying on Evie and she let me down. I know she was sorry; I know she did truly love Nanny Pat and I do love Evie dearly, but I have needed time to heal. I have needed so much time. Evie had visited me here in the past but everything she said just went in one ear and out the other, I wasn't listening; I was lost in a world of my own suffering, but now I was starting to come round. Had I rediscovered my zest for life? It was the first time I was actually looking forward to Evie's visit; how was the world out there? Before now I couldn't give a monkeys!

"Hello, dad. It is so wonderful to see you," said Evie, as she flung her arms around me. "I miss you; I want you back home."

"How is it living at Auntie Eileen's? Are you happy? Are you, Jodie and Lollypop all getting on?"

"We are, dad, we are fine," confirmed Evie, "but I want to be able to live with you again. I should be looking after you. The world out there is scary; I need to be with you. Have you been watching the news?"

"No, not really," I replied. "I haven't been interested; I've been too wrapped up in myself. What is it like out there?"

"It's horrible, dad," answered Evie, "especially in this country. Our Prime Minister, Fierce Morgan, has been going completely rogue. It has been so bad; the country has become a totalitarian state, a bit like North Korea. Around every street and every corner there is a poster of Fierce Morgan. He is everywhere and anybody on Twitter which debates with him is instantly jailed.

They said the jails have had to be quadrupled in the last two years. Fierce has said he is considering bringing back the death penalty for anybody that disagrees with him and he will, I am sure. I have to tell you, Fierce Morgan has been on Good Day Britain this morning, giving his latest decrees and the latest one is very serious."

"What's that?" I asked Evie.

"He is banning all religion and is getting his chief diplomat, Keven Peters to argue all around the world that every country should copy the UK. I am afraid Fierce is particularly keen on taking on God's Onlookers; he doesn't like being called Unrighteous. I can feel the world's end date coming very close; that is why you need to be with me. Please, dad, come home before its too late," pleaded Evie.

"It is certainly making me think, and yes, I want to be with you as you are a special loved one," I told her. "Have you got your powers back? Are you perfect again? I hated seeing you in distress seeing Nanny Pat die and seeing your perfection dissipate, but I didn't have any strength anymore; I was too ill to help you."

"I am fully myself again," said Evie happily. "I have had to be truly remorseful, which I was, and learn from my mistake, which I have. My perfection has been restored."

"I am so relieved," I replied.

"Come on, dad, you need to leave here," urged Evie. "Did you know most of the Arctic Polar Ice Cap has now broken away meaning lands are disappearing fast and the Earth is becoming scorched due to the climate change. You have to make the most of the time you have left on this Earth with me, not stuck in here. I am perfect again; I can teleport and I think its time you teleported with me. What do you think, dad?"

"I would love to, Evie," I admitted. "But how can I? I am a mere mortal; I am not capable of anything like that, am I?"

"But I am," said Evie. "And as long as you have a connection to me, like holding my hand, you can teleport with me. It would be like having an umbilical cord to me. Are you up for it? It is time to break the chains; we need to have some real adventures together before its too late. I can hear the New Order calling; its ringing loud and clear. It's coming closer."

"You've convinced me, Evie. I am out of here," I replied, realising the timetable of the world's demise was now coming much faster than I was told when I had previously been in the new order. Everything was not right about this world I was currently living in, It was never supposed to be like this! "let's go!, I urged her, "there really is no time like the present, no more time to waste.

"I am so glad you said that. I am so happy I could cry," said an emotional Evie. "You will be so glad you want to do it. You won't have any regrets; you will love it."

"Where do you propose to teleport us to?" I asked Evie. "Have you got a favourite spot in the world you want to go?"

"It's not where, dad. I told you the Earth is in a terrible state. I can sense a cosmic storm hitting this Earth in a short space of time. A lot of the Earth is becoming inhospitable, even nearby, like Spain, is far too unbearably hot now," revealed Evie.

"So, what then?" I asked her. "I am so confused."

"It is not where we teleport, dad. It is to what year we teleport," revealed Evie. "I can not only teleport anywhere, I can also teleport through time, I can give you three wishes; just think of three times in your life you would want to experience again and I can take you to that moment. We would be like bystanders as we watch; we won't be visible, we will be on a different plane of existence to the historical reality going on. It will be strange for you, as you will be seeing your younger self acting out naturally. You will be watching history unfold again. Can you think of your first memory you would like to return to and experience one more time for eternal posterity?"

"I can. It is in the year 1976, the summer of 1976. I was a 13 year old boy and had a best friend, Dek, who was two years older than me. I want to go back to me, Dek, my mum, my dad and my two sisters, Eileen and Louise, sitting in our indoor sauna. It is 9 pm at night, a lovely summer's night and we are all in the sauna ready to jump into our indoor swimming pool at El Campo. I want to see my mum and dad again and this was one of my greatest memories. Can we really do this, Evie?" I asked her.

"Yes, we can. It is a lovely memory; I am so excited," said Evie. "Just picture the scene clearly in your mind. Imagine you are there. Hold my hand and I will pick up what is in your mind and execute that image. You will be there; this is so exciting."

"I've got the image really vivid in my mind. I am ready to hold your hand for you to engage the image," I told her.

"Get ready; hold on to your hat, we're doing it," shouted Evie.

"This is amazing! This is a miracle! I can't believe it. I am so happy, Evie, thank you so much," I shrieked with emotion. "We are all sitting there in the sauna, mum, Eileen and Louise on the left-hand side and me, Dek and dad on the right-hand side. The steam rising in the sauna is intense. I remember that so well. Dad is putting even more water on the stove and it looks so hot in there everybody is sweating buckets. Dek is first out and he has jumped straight into the swimming pool. It is usually freezing, but Dek is so hot he is not feeling it. Louise is next, then it's me, then mum, then Eileen and lastly dad. We are all in the swimming pool. It is now dark outside but the pool room is illuminated. This is fantastic; this is such an iconic childhood memory, so thank you. Evie, are you crying?"

"I am sorry, father," cried Evie. "Seeing your mum again, my Nanny Pat, has made me cry. She looks so young again and your dad, that is how they will be in the New Order. This is so emotional, isn't it? And you are just a teenager. It I so weird seeing you like this.

You are having so much fun, as is your friend and your sisters. Wasn't it wonderful to have a swimming pool in your house? How lucky were you?"

"Very lucky. Dad did us proud; he worked so hard for us all," I told her. "Respect to dad."

"You all look like you haven't any cares in the world," observed Evie.

"At that precise moment we didn't," I agreed.

"It has been a brilliant memory," said Evie. "Are you ready for the next one?"

"Yes. I want us to go to April 10th 1987 at 7.45 pm in the evening, to the Maggie Stanley maternity unit. I want to witness the birth of my son, Dean, again," I answered. "It is in Derby. I want to remember probably the most stunning moment in my life seeing my son born, to realise I was actually a dad. Me, a dad! It felt surreal; it felt beyond my wildest dreams."

"That's beautiful, dad," commented Eve. "I am so happy I am going to see my big half-brother coming into this world. It is so beautiful. Are you ready to channel your mind and concentrate and focus intently? You are in that room and I will pick it up. Hold my hand, dad."

"Oh my God! I am in the maternity ward. This is so emotional I want to cry. My first wife is in bed; she is pushing like crazy. She is a very brave girl. I am glad us blokes don't have to go through this," I commented.

"I bet you are, dad," remarked Evie.

"She is screaming blue murder, isn't she? She says I'm a dead man if I do this to her again. I forgot that bit! The epidural is now beginning to work, thank goodness for that. I've noticed the clock says 8 pm at night; my son will be born in half an hour. He was born at 8.30 pm in the evening and I was the happiest man alive," I told Evie.

"I should think so, dad. You have every right to be. You look so excited, dad; it looks like you are going to faint," remarked Evie.

"I know. It was all so overwhelming as the time got near," I said.

"The midwife is telling your wife she can see the baby's head; She can see Dean's head. This is so emotional, isn't it? I can see tears of joy in your eyes; it is not long now," said Evie.

"Dean is being pushed out now. My baby is coming. I look ecstatic, don't I?" I remarked. "Just look at him; Dean is now in his mummy's arms; the midwife has passed him to her. They look beautiful together. My wife looks exhausted, doesn't she?" I remarked.

"No kidding, José, that is an understatement. I think if your pelvic floor had gone through such trauma, you would be just a little bit tired, don't you think?" mocked Evie.

"If my pelvic floor went through that, I would be in intensive care," I cringed with the thought. "Mummy and baby together; it truly is a miracle, isn't it?" A biological miracle, a biological act of wonder. It is a picture of pure bliss, a picture of total bliss. Can I ask you one more thing, Evie? While were in this moment of time, are you able to fast forward to the following morning?" I asked her.

"Yes," she replied.

"I want to see myself returning to the maternity ward in the morning to collect my ex-wife and my new baby, Dean, to take them home. It was 10 am in the morning; it was a Sunday morning. I want to see myself clapping eyes on my new baby son looking so cute all wrapped up ready to come home. The thing that I can always remember is seeing how chilled out he looked. He didn't cry at all. The maternity staff said that of all the babies born in the ward that weekend, Dean was by far the most relaxed. Dean was the biggest sleepy head of them all," I reminisced. "I had to pinch myself all this wasn't a crazy dream. I had to realise my son was really born; I really was a dad."

Evie duly let me have that cherished memory as an added bonus. It was time to have my third memory; it was June 2003, my wedding day to Amy Jane.

"Amy Jane looks so beautiful, dad. I love her wedding dress. She looks so radiant. She looks divine," remarked Evie.

"She would look beautiful in any setting," I said. "Amy Jane was special; she was my true love."

"You have spruced up well, dad," remarked Evie. "You look very smart in your suit. You look handsome."

"Well thank you," I replied to her.

"Your mum and dad and your two sisters look so happy for you and aah, look at Jodie and Lollypop; they are so little. Aren't they just the cutest things in their bridesmaids dresses. I love the white flowers they have in their hair, the white roses. It makes me want to get married one day," admitted Evie.

"Now look at me, I am repeating the marriage vows. I look so nervous, don't I? I am trembling with nerves; I can hear the vicar saying 'for richer for poorer' and my lips look so dry," I observed.

"Look at the way Amy Jane is looking at you," said Evie. "She so loves you. She is so happy I think I am going to cry."

"I am putting the ring on her finger now," I observed. "This is so emotional. I am kissing the bride; I am kissing Amy Jane."

"The bells are ringing; confetti is going everywhere. You and Amy Jane are man and wife. Congratulations," said Evie. "It is time to leave all this behind I am afraid. We need to return to the present. Please hold my hand, dad. I want us to go to my place now; it is time, dad." Urged Evie.

"What do you mean, it's time?" I asked her, feeling very puzzled.

"It is time for me to return," answered Evie, cryptically. "I can sense the bad man is coming. I can sense the bad man's presence. It is time; please hold my hand, dad."

"Is he here at my wedding? Surely not," I replied, feeling very anxious.

"No, dad, he is waiting for us back in the present. It is time to face him," said Evie.

"I do not like the sound of that," I replied. "Are we heading back to Derby?"

"No," answered Evie. "It is going to be a surprise."

What surprise did Evie have in mind? Where were we heading? Wherever it was, it sounded like the bad man was not going to be too far away. It sounded very ominous, like the bad man was now after me, and Evie wanted to confront him head on. What made her so confident, if that was the case, she could resist him? Was Evie going to try and protect me from him? How could she? The bad man was a very bad man and very powerful; could he be overcome? Was Evie taking me to meet my doom? In one way it was still a merciful release if it wasn't too painful for me. I had enjoyed three fantastic last hurrahs if this was the case, all thanks to my wonderful daughter, Evie. My gifted daughter had provided me with three of my most cherished memories as she turned back time and allowed me to witness how happy I could be and that my life, if it was to end imminently, was ultimately not a bad life at all. I did have many blessings; I needed to be so grateful to my gifted daughter to be reminded of that, instead of wallowing in the black gloom of the world's current and present precarious predicament. Thank you so much, Evie. If I do leave this mortal coil, I will miss you so much!

CHAPTER 14

THE BEGINNING OF THE END

"So where are we, Evie? I don't recognise this place. Where are we? It is all dark; it is nighttime and it is so cold. We are surrounded by snow. Are we on a glacier?"

"We are at the North Pole," replied Evie. "And yes, we are on a glacier. It is only one of a few left due to all the global warming and it is nighttime for a reason. I am here for a reason; this is my place, my rightful place at this moment in time."

"What reason?" I asked her. "Why are we here?"

"We are here to see the Northern Lights. This is what I want. This is what I need to do. The Aurora Borealis is going to be extra special tonight. That is why we are here," disclosed Evie.

"It all sounds good," I said. "It sounds spectacular. I have always wanted to see such a show, an amazing light show."

"They are going to be even more special tonight," revealed Evie. "The sun has just produced a very strong geomagnetic storm, caused by a huge eruption on the surface of the sun. All this has created a huge solar wind and the Aurora Borealis is going to be spectacular as a result when it is produced because of this surge of solar wind meeting the Earth's atmosphere. This is going to provide an extraordinary display of colour; you will see large areas of green, pink, red, yellow, blue and violet in the sky. It will appear high in the sky, but it might appear it is coming towards you in the form of a spectacular giant multi-coloured wave. It is so beautiful."

"I am excited; I can even see an Eskimo in the near distance. He has come to watch it as well, hasn't he? He looks well wrapped up and protected from the elements. His hoodie is down; I bet he sees a lot of these events, doesn't he?"

"That is not an Eskimo," revealed Evie. "It's the bad man. The bad man is here, Winston is here. The Aurora Borealis will be appearing any minute now; are you ready, dad?"

"Aren't you bothered the bad man is here?" I shouted. "It usually results in death. Aren't you bothered, Evie?"

"No," she replied.

"Why not?" I asked her. "Aren't you worried the bad man is coming for me? Aren't you worried Winston is about to kill your dad? I guess I am well and truly done for now. Oh well, it's been a blast. I just hope Winston lets me see the light show before he kills me. Is that too much to ask? I hope not."

"The bad man is not here for you," revealed Evie. "You can relax, dad."

"Phew!" I said, before coming to the horrific conclusion.

"So why is the bad man here? Oh no, he is here for you, isn't he, Evie? Oh no, please don't let this happen. We have to leave, Evie, we have to leave at once!" I urged her, in a blind panic.

"No, dad," said Evie. "It is my time. Don't worry about the bad man; once I am gone he will leave you alone, I promise you that. The bad man is here to watch the lights. Oh look, the lights are here. They are magnificent, aren't they? They are so mesmerising; they are hypnotic. They are truly beautiful, they are ......"

"I know they are but I don't understand all this," I interrupted.

"You need to let go of my hand now, dad. The bad man won't hurt you," encouraged Evie. "Look, the lights have completely filled the sky; it is so wondrous."

"It really is wondrous," I said, as I let go of her hand.

"Aren't they beautiful? They are moving so fast. The lights are coming down towards us, dad. Make sure you have let go of my hand, or ....."

"Or what?" I asked. "What are you not telling me?"

"The lights have come for me. It is my time. I love you, dad, and always will. I am not supposed to live on this

Earth at this time; I was never supposed to live on this Earth at this time, but I am so glad I did. I am so glad to have had this human experience with you as my dad. I would have wanted no other person to share my time on this Earth with. I love you so dearly. I am going forward to the New Order, God's New Order. That is where all the perfect ones are, just like me. You know I don't belong here in this imperfect world, surrounded by imperfect humans. I have to go; the lights have come to take me away. Please be happy for me, dad. I will miss you so much," stated Evie.

"You mustn't go, Evie," I begged. "You are the only thing left worth living for. You are my precious daughter. I don't want to go on living without you. Please don't do this to me, Evie."

"I have to; it's my time. I have to return to the promised New Order. I can't stay on this Earth any longer or my future existence would be in grave peril. You have to leave me now; the lights are nearly enveloping us. You must leave the light, dad, or ...."

"Or what? What will happen, Evie?" I argued. "What's going to happen?"

"The lights will take you with me. You will die; you will be taken from this Earth and put into a peaceful rest while the New Order is finally established. Please go, dad, this is serious," urged Evie. "You don't have long."

"I am not going anywhere," I protested. "We leave this world together. There is nothing left to live for; the bad man has made sure of that. He has taken my mum, my son, my greatest love and now you're leaving me. The world is in tatters; my world is in tatters. I have not got the strength in me to cope with the end of the world when it comes and anyway, could you bear to live in a country run by Fierce Morgan?"

"No. You do have a point there," admitted Evie. "Are you sure you know what you are doing, dad? There is no going back. It is almost totally done now; the lights around us are extensive. Have you made one last wish?" urged Evie. "Look, have you noticed the bad man watching us through the light around us?"

"He is giving us the thumbs up, isn't he?" I answered. "What is he trying to say?"

"You do the maths, dad. The bad man is from Death itself and for the time being that is where you're heading. The bad man's work is done. Look, he has vanished. There is no escape from this light now, dad. Your fate and mine are sealed. Have you noticed the change in the light, dad?" asked Evie.

"Yes, I have," I answered. "The spectrum of colour it was emitting has gone and become a brilliant white light. It is so piercing; it feels so powerful and it feels like we are rising with it."

"Goodbye, dad. Rest well. I love you forever and for eternity. Remember, somewhere, somehow, we will meet again. Goodbye, dad."

Evie's words were beautiful and something to behold. Tears were going to be permanently etched onto my face as I headed inexorably towards peace and rest. My fate, along with every other individual on this Earth, alive or dead, now laid in God's hands. Was I one of the selfless to live again, or the selfish that wouldn't? God was the judge. At least I didn't have to live through the end of the world; now that was scary! My eyes closed for the last time. I hoped I had done enough; I hoped I had been good enough, but I did know living my life had been a blast!! Paul Jackson R.I.P.

I wasn't to know it, but the skewed world I had awoken in had been put right at a stroke. It was mine and Evie's departure from this broken world that had allowed the original timeline to reset. The world was again now due to end in the year 2033. My dad was still alive, albeit in a very poorly state, but would live until the year 2010. My mum did get bowel cancer in 2016, but I was glad to say made a full recovery, God willing! Thankfully there was no Winston as the anaesthetist to jeopardise her health. My son, Dean, did go in the army at the age of 16 and thankfully wasn't shot by friendly fire and Laura did, unfortunately, meet her demise in November 2000. Mum was, and still is, one of God's Onlookers; she does firmly believe God is coming and that the world is in a right state. Who could possibly argue with her?

We don't have Fierce Morgan as Prime Minister, so thank goodness this other world didn't happen, although could he be any worse than the politicians we have? I'll let you be the judge of that. Maybe there was something to be said for this other world, after all! Normality had been restored, or had it?

CHAPTER 15

THE STING IN THE TALE

1st October 2000, 12 pm, Royal Derby Hospital

"Again! Again! He is not responding! Again! I can't detect any heartbeat. Again!" urged the emergency nurse. "There is no pulse. Let's try one more time. Again!, Again!, It's no good; Mr Jackson has made no response. The Defibrillator hasn't worked. We haven't been able to resuscitate him. I am so sorry, I pronounce Mr Paul Jackson dead. Please record his time of death as the 1st October, 2000 at 12.01 pm."

"Dad! Dad! I love you, dad!" cried Dean hysterically. "I've lost my dad! I can't stand it; this is unbearable! What am I going to do without my dad? Please come back to us; don't go, please don't go."

"He's gone, love. Your dad's gone. He is at rest now," comforted mum. "He will be alright; he will live again. I feel it in my being."

"I can't believe dad's gone. He seemed alright last night, didn't he?" said Dean. "It's why I can't believe he's gone. What on Earth was he going on about last night?

Do you think he was delirious when he kept talking about that New Order, Nan?"

"Maybe, but he sounded serious and coherent to me," answered mum. "I loved the sound of it, I would love to be young again, I'll buy that."

"It was right weird, if you ask me," complained Dean. "How are we going to break the news to Amy Jane? She was floating on air last night. Dad proposed to her. She is going to be absolutely devastated. I don't know how she is going to take this bad news. Is she at work?"

"Yes. I am not looking forward to when she finds out. She was hysterical until he woke up last night and now this. It is so cruel; life can be so cruel sometimes. You are given something one day and then it's snatched away again. The only tiny crumb of comfort is Amy Jane knew Paul wanted to marry her before he passed away. We have got to tell your grandad the bad news as well. He is so frail, I hope this doesn't finish him off," said mum.

Do you think any of dad's predictions will come true?" Dean asked his Nan. "You know, the Smartphone thingy; the Googly thingy? I hope it does."

"It will be so interesting to find out, that's for sure," answered mum, "because if that comes true it could mean all the other things he mentioned could come true and if they do, your dad will see us again in the future. We will meet again one day!"

With that, they said their last goodbyes with the most precious commodity humans can have ...., hope! What are we without hope?

This was the nicer ending, an ending fit for lovers of the light, but! (If you like the Shade, read on .....)

10 years later. Dean and Amy Jane's wedding

"Oh, Dean, you have made me the happiest girl in the world. I love you; I can't believe I have just become your wife," said Amy Jane.

"I know. It feels just such a beautiful thing," agreed Dean. "Me and you, man and wife."

"If you hadn't spotted me on Facebook, I hate to think where I would be now," said Amy Jane. "You saved my life that day and to think that was only two years ago. It seems like a whole different lifetime ago."

"It does," agreed Dean. "Can you remember my dad that night before he died in his hospital bed? He came out with all sorts of things, didn't he? He said you would become hooked on this thing called Facebook and he was right. How many friends do you have on it now, Amy Jane?"

"Last time I looked it was over 1,500," answered Amy Jane.

"I think that has proved my dad right," confirmed Dean.

"I wonder if your dad was watching us today from up above in the sky?" asked Amy Jane. "How do you think he would be feeling seeing me married to his son? He did ask me to marry him just before he died, so part of me can't help feeling guilty. Do you think he is happy for us, Dean?"

"I hope so, I sincerely hope so," Dean answered. "I am so sorry he is not here to see me get married. Any son would want their dad to be there at his wedding; but maybe it is better he is resting in peace, as the sight of you being my wife, I could imagine would be very traumatic for him, I guess."

"Do you think your dad will ever live again? He did seem so positive that he had lived again and he had met us in that New Order. He kept going on about that, didn't he? He sounded so convincing," said Amy Jane.

"Who knows?" answered Dean. "But if dad is right, I suppose it will feel very awkward indeed, won't it?"

"Are you going to tell me where you're taking me on honeymoon now, Dean?" asked Amy Jane. "You know I hate surprises. Is it somewhere nice and sunny? Please say it is."

"It is nice and sunny," confirmed Dean. "It is Barbados. We are going to the Caribbean; how's that for you? Is that warm enough for you?"

"That's great," said an excited Amy Jane.

"I am glad you said that," replied Dean. "Because the taxi will be here soon. You have an hour to pack and then it is our dream break on a paradise beach."

"That's so wonderful. You do know how to make a girl happy, don't you? Thank you so much, Mr Dean Jackson, my new beloved husband," sighed Amy Jane.

"It is a pleasure to see you so excited and happy, Mrs Jackson. I am so happy you are now my wife. We have so much to live for and we now do it together. You better hurry up and pack, as you know how indecisive you can be," encouraged Dean.

One hour later

"Taxi's here! Are you ready, Amy Jane?" called out Dean.

"I'm coming, I'm coming, finally done, I think," replied Amy Jane.

"Where do you want to go, Mr Jackson?" asked the taxi driver.

"To the airport, please," confirmed Dean. "Birmingham airport, please."

"Let's get your luggage in the back, then," replied the taxi driver. "Cor blimey, that's heavy."

"I'm sorry. That is Amy Jane for you" sighed Dean. "She has put everything in it apart from the kitchen sink, hasn't she?"

"A girl has to be prepared," remarked Amy Jane.

"Let's go," urged the taxi driver, "before I develop a hernia."

"Ooh, you are funny," commented Amy Jane. "That was a joke, wasn't it?"

"So, is this a special trip?" asked the taxi driver. "Are you heading for anywhere nice?"

"We have just got married, so it is our honeymoon. We are flying to Barbados. It is going to be so special for us, something we can remember for the rest of our lives," answered Dean.

"Yes, I am so excited! I can't wait to be in my bikini and swim in the turquoise sea and sunbathe under the palm trees on a hot and sandy beach," remarked a very joyful Amy Jane.

"I agree with that. I can't wait to be on that hot and sunny beach with you," confirmed Dean.

"It sounds amazing. I am almost jealous of you two," commented the taxi driver, who by now had missed the obvious turn for getting to the airport and that hadn't gone unnoticed by Dean.

"You've missed the turn there, mate. I hope you know what you are doing, as we don't want to miss the deadline for the check in," he warned.

The taxi driver didn't answer. He had become mute all of a sudden.

"Are you listening to me? You are going the wrong way. What are you doing? What are you playing at?" said an increasingly agitated Dean. "Either turn around or stop the car. Stop the car!!"

"I don't like this; I don't like this at all," cried Amy Jane. "Why is the taxi driver not listening to us? Why is he not talking to us?"

"He's locked the back door; we're locked in," shouted Dean. "Oi, mate, I don't know what your game is but you are totally out of order. When you stop, I am going to punch your lights out and make sure you are fired. Do you get me?"

"Let us out!" cried Amy Jane. "I'm scared!"

"Please try to calm down." The taxi driver suddenly began to speak again as the taxi joined the M5.

"Where are you taking us? Where the hell are you taking us?" Dean demanded to know.

"I think the Avon Gorge is nice this time of year, don't you agree?" Replied the taxi driver. "Especially if you can see it close to the edge in a very fast car."

"Let us out; let us out now!" shouted Dean.

"Let us out!" screamed Amy Jane.

"I think you need to be less rude," commented the taxi driver. "You need to be more civil and more appreciative.

Start talking to me with a bit more respect; you haven't even asked me what my name is."

"What is your name?" asked a very tearful Amy Jane. "I promise we will talk to you nicely from now on. Just please let us go."

"Yes. If you let us go, we can forget all about this. We are sorry if we have offended you," said Dean. "Just tell us your name and we will talk nicely to you."

"My name is ….., my name is Winston and I am a bad man, a very bad man!!"

EPILOGUE

This was the mystery to end all mysteries. Why was the bad man still around and once again targeting my loved ones? The world was supposed to be properly reset and back to normal following my passing; a world where Dean and Amy Jane got married but both lived to survive the Great War in the last days. But now, following the bad man's intervention, they were destined to die together at the bottom of Avon Gorge. This was not supposed to happen; this was not supposed to happen at all?

What it all meant was Dean and Amy Jane were no longer necessarily going to be married in the now rewritten New Order, as Death had parted them, so their marriage vows had been amongst the shortest in history. There was no longer an obligation under God to be married to each other when they both got to be reborn into God's new world, something that Death had intervened with through the bad man. The mystery remained, why? Who could benefit from this tragic course of events? The only hint that could be gleamed was a very seemingly innocent and innocuous remark from Evie in the Northern Lights when we were completely cloaked in it. She asked me if I had made a last wish. I thought it was strange, but harmless; why not indulge yourself with a last wish when you were heading for Death's door? What harm could it do?

I made a wish, a wish that came straight from my aching heart. I wanted to be able to marry and stay married to the person I loved the most, Amy Jane, if I was ever lucky to live again. That was my fervent wish, something that was denied to me in the original New Order and led me to seeking the love of the wrong person for me and Evie's introduction into a world she should never have frequented. Was this time's way of untying all the knots? If so, it was very cruel. I would never have wanted to be responsible for Dean and Amy Jane's demise, but to my horror I suddenly realised and remembered Evie's following comment following my wish. "*Look, have you noticed the bad man watching us through the light?*"

I had. He was giving us the thumbs up. He was giving me the thumbs up to my last wish. I had given the bad man a chance for a last hurrah; Amy Jane could be a free girl after all. The New Order would now be different next time around, but how different?

THE END

AFTERWORD

It is the sincerest wish of this author that you enjoyed this largely fictitious piece of work. It was all written with the best of motives and in good faith in directing you to what the Bible actually says about living again. When this novel was written it was with my current understanding at that time regarding resurrection and living again. I have since developed further understanding on this subject and this will come out in my next novel, ITS THEM AGAINST US! (We'll meet again 2).

Not everything in this novel was imaginary. The lead character, Mr Paul Jackson, was based on myself and I was indeed involved in a car crash on the 30th September 2003.(I changed the year to 2000 in my novel for creative purposes) I was wearing a seat belt and survived a very nasty incident. I was a flower delivery driver and was being ferried around that day by the boyfriend of my lady boss, who did indeed panic when he missed a turn into Alrewas. All this is true and set up the perfect premise for my novel and that was, what if I hadn't been wearing my seat belt? I could have died that day! The impact on our car was considerable enough to spin it around ninety degrees. I was really shook up but very grateful to be alive, albeit with a horrible whiplash. It did make me think how precious life is, but if it was to be curtailed early, was that it? Or was there more to come, a better life?

My childhood association with a religious group called the Jehovah's Witnesses had already given me an indication there was going to be a time in the future when all the people who have died will live again (*John 5 verses 21-30*). This was my motivation in writing this novel, to try and give comfort and make the reader aware of what the Bible says, especially when good people were dying through Covid.

The character of Dean in this novel really is based on my son. I do have a son called Dean and he did go into the army after leaving school. My mum really is religious, a lifelong pioneer, and unfortunately my dad did pass away in the year 2010. I miss him a lot and respect him greatly for how he provided for us. Amy Jane is, unfortunately for me, a fictional character, but was based on a girl I was so deeply in love with a few years ago that was already in a loving relationship. It was so easy to write and express my feelings for this character, as was Laura, another person I had strong feelings for who did have a young daughter which inspired the character of Evie. It made this novel so easy to piece together. They say life imitates art, don't they?

There is a serious message in this novel, in that I do honestly think we are living in perilous times and that the direction of travel is only leading one way and that is the end times. I personally hope I will be peacefully at rest by then, just like my character, Paul Jackson, was in my novel, as it is scary just how the majority of the world is behaving, but I do know why and how it will end. You just have to make sure you want to be on the right side and that is to love God, to love Jesus Christ. That is the only way! (*John 14.6*).

I am no longer a Jehovah's Witness, as I developed some serious doubts, but I do consider myself a Christian, or at least a person that strives to be a good person and a respecter of truth. My understanding of the Bible is different to how I was as a child and continues to evolve, but the ethos of this novel remains. We will live again; we'll meet again.

DEDICATION

(John Stant 1933–2010)

(My inspiration to write and to try and succeed in life. This work is dedicated to you. Life is too short not to try, we all have to try and fulfil our potential. XX.)

This novel is dedicated to the memory of my late father. Thank you for everything you did for us. One day I have hope we'll meet again! X.

Milton Keynes UK
Ingram Content Group UK Ltd.
UKHW010303260524
443077UK00002B/6